ALSO BY AMANDA HAMM

WEATHERING EVAN

THE 4TH FLOOR LOUNGE

MEET CUTE: 5 ROMANTIC SHORT STORIES

THE STORIES FROM HARTFORD SERIES
ANDREW'S KEY
JEALOUSY & YAMS
COLLECTING ZEBRAS
THE CHRISTMAS PROJECT
HEARTS ON THE WINDOW (EBOOK NOVELLA)

THE COFFEE AND DONUTS SERIES
SAID AND UNSAID
SOFIE WAITS
A PERFECTLY GOOD MAN
NOT COMPLICATED

They See a Family

Amanda Hamm

ISBN: 978-1943598502

They See a Family is a work of fiction. All names, characters, places, events, etc.
are products of the author's imagination or are used fictitiously.

1

Kay was babysitting when she got the call. She needed to get to the hospital. But she was babysitting. She had no car seats for the little ones. She couldn't drive to the hospital without car seats. Her first thought was to go to the store on the way so she could buy car seats. But she couldn't drive to the store either. Her brain swirled around what seemed an impossible problem. She couldn't leave home without car seats, and she couldn't get car seats without leaving home.

It couldn't be real. Kay felt overpowered by the situation and needed someone to rescue her. William. William could bring her car seats. She fished in her purse for her phone while the infant in her other arm began to fuss. "Shh," she whispered. "I'm gonna take care of both of you. Just hang on a minute." She lightly bounced her arm up and down as she waited for William to answer.

"Kay. How'd the babysitting go?"

"I need help."

"Two under two is a bit much to handle, huh?"

"No, I really need help. They were in an accident. I need to go to the hospital, but I don't have car seats. Can you go to the store and buy car seats and bring them to me? I'll pay you back."

"Whoa. Slow down." His tone became serious and business-like. "Rob and Beth were in an accident?"

"Yeah. I need to go, and I'm stuck here with the babies."

"Couldn't I just come over and watch them for you?"

"No. No, I need to take them because…" She couldn't say it. She couldn't say out loud that when her sister found out her husband was dead – if she didn't know already – she would need to hold her babies. They would get her through this. "I just need car seats."

"How old are they exactly?"

"Two months and thirteen months."

"Two months and thirteen months." William seemed to be repeating the ages to commit them to memory. "Okay. I'll call Annie from the store. She can tell me what you need. I'll be there as soon as I can."

"Thanks." Kay hung up and dropped her phone on the counter. Pete had worked himself into a full wail while they talked. She pulled him into her chest and held him. "Time for that bottle Mommy left for you." She pulled the bottle from the fridge and gave it a little shake. The milk had separated somewhat.

"Here we go." She sat with Pete on her couch and positioned him in the crook of her arm. His brother, Will, was sitting on the floor playing with the laces on a pair of Kay's shoes. She held the nipple in his mouth, wiggling it against his bottom lip, and he continued to cry. "Here it is," she whispered soothingly. He turned his head away and cried harder.

"Oh, you're used to it warm, aren't you? Sorry, sweetie, I'm a little scattered at the moment. I know I should warm it." Kay shook her head, trying to focus, as she returned to the kitchen. Beth had said something about not putting it in the microwave. Kay turned hot water on at the sink and held the bottle under it.

Will crawled after her to see what was going on. She smiled at him; he smiled back. Then she put her attention on the bottle. She was trying to calm Pete with some jiggles, and it wasn't doing any good. Every time she pulled the bottle out of the stream of water, the milk inside seemed just as cold as when she started.

2

A whimper made her look back at Will. His face was scrunched up in the beginning of a cry. For no reason she could see. "No." Kay shook her head. "Don't cry. Everything's fine. There's no reason to cry." She offered him an encouraging smile.

Apparently, he didn't believe her because he burst into real tears. And why should he believe her? She was lying to him. Everything wasn't fine. His father was dead. His life was forever changed. His aunt was incapable of even warming up a bottle. Between the two crying babies and the rushing water, Kay felt everything in her already tiny apartment begin to shrink. No wonder Beth had looked so happy when she left for a night out.

Kay took a deep breath. She shut off the water and set down the bottle. She crouched on the floor and patted Will's back. She couldn't pick them both up without risking dropping one. Will settled somewhat with the attention. She looked desperately around the room for something to entertain him, something that would keep him busy while she figured out how to feed the smaller baby.

Perhaps he'd like to bang on a pot. She reached over and opened a lower cabinet. Before she could pull out a pot, Will's little hands slapped across the floor to grab the door. He sat up and opened and closed it several times as though it was the most fascinating thing he'd ever seen. All the cabinets at Rob and Beth's house had latches. There probably was some novelty to doors that opened freely.

How much time it would give her to deal with Pete she didn't know. She picked up the bottle again. It seemed to have at least gotten to room temperature. Maybe that was good enough. She held the nipple in Pete's mouth and moved it around, trying to get him to start sucking. He was frantic and still ignoring the food.

She set the bottle down yet again and tipped Pete up to her shoulder and bounced him as she walked in a circle. Surely he'd take the bottle if she could get him to calm down a little first. He did begin to quiet and soon she realized he had cried himself to sleep. That was fine. The bottle could wait. But should it wait in the refrigerator? Kay didn't want to have to start over warming it. How long could it sit out and not spoil? Beth referred to breast milk as liquid gold. That felt appropriate as Kay looked at less than four ounces of milk and knew it was the only thing in her entire place she could feed to her nephew.

Maybe she should have asked William to buy formula, too. Maybe they should get some on the way to the hospital. Kay didn't know anything about Beth's injuries. What if she'd been given medication that would prevent her from nursing? They should buy formula just in case. At least that would come with instructions.

Will had moved on to another cupboard to see if it opened, too. Kay's kitchen was peaceful for the moment. She closed her eyes in prayer. "Please, God, let Beth be okay. Help her to cope with this loss. Give me the strength to help her. She won't be alone with these babies. We'll both help her."

Pete sighed heavily and shifted in her arms. Kay tried to imagine God holding her like she held the baby. She breathed a little easier but felt too much tension to let it all out the way Pete had. She was calm enough to be practical though. She went back to her phone and texted William to buy formula. Then she paced her apartment, hoping the movement would keep Pete asleep.

He was still sleeping on her shoulder when William arrived. The huge box in his hands barely fit through her doorway. He dropped it on the floor and smiled at Will like he was delivering a gift. "This is for you."

His demeanor became more serious as he addressed Kay. "When I called Annie, she said they had an infant seat their youngest has outgrown that you could have. She even drove to the store with it so I'd only have to make one stop. The next time I complain about my sister, you can remind me of this." He paused to give a friendly wave to Will, who had backed himself to the far side of the room and was staring at William. Then he ripped open the box. He pulled out a gray car seat and sat on the floor next to it with an instruction booklet. He tore off some plastic and threw some tags to the side. "Sorry I'm making a mess."

"I'm not worried about that right now." Kay's voice trembled and she jiggled Pete a little faster, as though he was the one who needed comfort.

William nodded briskly and returned his attention to the car seat. He turned a few pages in the instructions, tilted the seat back, fussed with the straps. He looked at Will and frowned. "All right, buddy, you're probably not going to like this, but I need to measure you." He got up, trying to force a reassuring smile.

Will tucked himself into a ball as William approached, clearly not wanting the strange man to pick him up. His legs quivered as William put his hands under his arms and carried him to the car seat.

William spoke to him calmly, telling him it would only take a few seconds and how he'd get to ride in the seat soon. He marked the height of the baby's shoulder in the seat, nodded to himself, then set Will back on the floor. He went to work threading the straps.

Will quickly crawled to Kay and wrapped his little arms around her ankles as Pete woke up again. The infant squirmed and thrashed. He was working up the energy for another screaming fit. Kay pulled her leg free of Will and rushed to the kitchen, hoping she could get the bottle in Pete's mouth before he started crying. It didn't work. The baby still wouldn't take the bottle, and his brother started crying because she'd walked away from him.

Kay sat on the floor at the edge of the kitchen. She set Pete on her legs so that his head rested in the crook of her elbow and held the bottle in the same hand, aiming it more or less at his mouth. She held the other arm out to Will as he crawled onto her other leg. The older baby settled against her, but the smaller one became more frantic. She bounced her knee under him and tried to convince him that what was in the bottle was the same thing he got from his mom. It just had a different shape.

"Can I do anything?" William had paused in adjusting the car seat. His eyes looked at Kay with equal parts sympathy and helplessness.

"You are helping," Kay said. "Just get us in the car. I think they both want their mommy."

He nodded again. His eyes didn't immediately return to the instructions though. Instead, he asked, "How bad is it?"

Kay knew he meant the accident. She was too busy juggling babies to think of a softer way to deliver the news. "Rob's dead," she said.

William gasped. The shocked expression on his face somehow made the situation more real.

Kay fought hard against something that threatened to be a very ugly cry. She'd never get Pete calm if she lost control of herself.

The instruction booklet crinkled in William's hand as he threw it into the car seat. He stood and yanked the car seat off the floor. Two metal buckles clinked together as they dangled from either end of a strap hanging out the back. "I'm going to get this installed," he said, "then I'll come back with the infant one."

Little Will started crying again as the door closed. "Make up your mind," Kay mumbled. "You didn't like William and now you're mad that he's gone?" She rubbed his back. "Can you help me feed Pete? Do you want to hold the bottle?"

He either didn't understand or wasn't interested. He just cried. Pete was wailing so hard that silent gasps interrupted his cry and valuable milk was dripping down his chin, not his throat.

"This isn't working." Kay shifted Will off her lap and set down the bottle. She stood with the baby and laid his head against her shoulder. "Come with me." She motioned Will to follow her and he did, still crying. She pulled a pan out of her cupboard and set it on the floor. She grabbed a wooden spoon, tapped on the bottom to give Will the idea, then tried to hand it to him.

Will stopped crying, which was something. He didn't seem to have any interest in the spoon though. He crawled past it to the cupboard where Kay had gotten the pan. He opened it and began to pull all the other pans onto the floor.

While he was busy, Kay focused on Pete again. His cries were beginning to hurt her, not her ears but something inside that wanted to help him and couldn't. "Why won't you eat?" She held him in front of her and tried to look into his eyes. They were shut tight in the effort of crying. "Should we check your diaper?"

She hated to put him down while he cried, but Kay gently laid him on the carpet to open his jammies for an investigation. She squeezed the outside of the diaper. It didn't feel wet, but she got a fresh one on him anyway. Then she scooped him up again and tried again to get him to suck on the bottle.

She knew he hadn't yet taken a bottle. That wasn't supposed to be a problem though. Beth had fed him right before she left. They were only supposed to be gone around two hours. The bottle was a just in case that shouldn't have been necessary. But the two-month-old had now gone four hours without eating. He should be hungry enough to want it. He arched his back and stubbornly turned away from the artificial nipple.

Kay picked up the bib around his neck and dabbed at his

chin. The cloth was soaked. She unsnapped it and dropped it on the floor. There was a burp rag somewhere.

Will had a small saucepan and was using both his hands to lift and drop it against another pan. The repeated metal on metal made an awful clanging noise. But he was smiling. That made the noise bearable to Kay. She was picking up the burp rag when William returned through her front door.

"I think we're ready," he said. "Annie thinks she got this one about right for a two-month-old. He held up an infant carrier. It was covered in pink plaid, but Pete was much too young to care about using something designed for a girl. Kay glanced at the green carrier he'd arrived in. She didn't have the base it snapped into and wondered if that had been damaged in the accident. Pete might have to get used to the pink one. But the crash had also stolen his dad – he wouldn't even have memories of Rob – so a car seat seemed like an insignificant loss.

Kay bent over the plaid car seat with the baby and looked up at William. "Can you get Will buckled for me?"

"Sure."

She tried to push Pete's arms under the straps as gently as she could with him fighting her. He was still crying but with less intensity. It was almost as though he'd given up trying to tell her anything. She hoped he was sleepy and would fall asleep in the car. Beth could feed him soon after they arrived. God willing.

Surprisingly, Will was still smiling as William carried him out the door. It took Kay forever to warm up to new people and Will looked comfortable after ten minutes. She tried to be grateful and not jealous. Less crying was a good thing at the moment. It was a good thing at any moment. She clicked the buckles between Pete's tiny legs and stood as she thought of what she needed.

There was a grocery bag on the floor near the car seat box

with a can of formula showing through the plastic. William had evidently gotten her text in time. She grabbed that, stuffed it in the diaper bag Beth left. Then she grabbed her purse and the diaper bag and baby carrier. She set everything down on the landing to lock her door before she picked it all up again and made her way down the stairs.

She rented the top half of a duplex. There was a small parking lot off an alley behind the house, which was where her car was. But William was standing near the street, next to his car, and Will was in the back seat.

Kay approached him with confusion. She assumed he was putting the car seats in her car.

He appeared to understand her puzzled expression. "I'll drive you," he said.

He sort of had to since moving the car seats would be a huge hassle. Kay just nodded and snapped Pete's seat into its base. She sent a quick wave to Will, eyes flitting rapidly around the unfamiliar car.

"Which hospital?" William asked as he pulled his own seat belt into position.

"St. Charles."

He nodded and started the car.

2

"Do you know anything about how your sister's doing?"

Kay shook her head sadly. Not knowing was hard. What if no one had told her about Rob? What if they had, and she was all alone? Beth and Rob had a beautiful relationship. They'd met in college. They dated more than three years before they got married so no one could say they rushed into it. Beth's heart had rushed though. She'd called Kay after her first date with Rob and told her sister that she'd enjoyed the evening with her future husband.

Tears sprang to Kay's eyes as she thought about the two of them on their wedding day and when they announced they were expecting – both times – and so many other happy times. She was still getting to know Rob and now she would have to save what memories she had.

"Do you know what happened?" William's voice interrupted the flood of memories. Probably only a second before the tears would have fallen freely.

"Someone ran a red light. That's all I know. Rob was dead at the scene. Beth was taken... I was the top contact in Beth's... Oh, no! I wonder if someone called my dad. Or Rob's parents. I haven't..." Kay thought about calling her dad. She'd been so focused on trying to get to the hospital and a little frazzled by the babies. "Would it be better to wait until I actually know something before I call my dad? I mean, since he can't be here anyway."

William blew out a puff of air and winced. "I'm not sure there's a right answer. We'll be there soon though. Hopefully, we'll know something soon."

"Yeah." The back seat was quiet. "Maybe Pete went to sleep again. I hope he can wait until... Oh, no! I left his bottle on the counter. It'll go to waste. And I brought the formula and nothing to put it in. Someday, I'm going to be the worst mother."

"Kay..." William sent her a worried glance. "Don't beat yourself up. This is a difficult and unexpected situation. We'll figure something... There are babies at a hospital, right? Surely there are bottles. And I can go buy some if we can't get our hands on one."

Kay tried to calm down. The way he kept saying *we* helped. William wasn't just a ride to the hospital. He was going to stick by her side until she didn't need him anymore. "Thanks for coming to get me and... everything."

"I... you're welcome." He squirmed visibly in response to gratitude.

That felt very typical and in spite of everything else going on, it made a small smile flash on Kay's face. "Why does it always look like you're welcome is hard to say?"

"Only to you."

"You don't like it when I thank you for something?"

He sighed. "I worry you'll catch on to my ulterior motives for being nice."

An ulterior motive for being nice? That sounded like a joke. It wasn't a time for jokes, and William looked completely serious. Kay was quiet long enough that it would have been weird to say something anyway. She simply turned and looked out the window.

They were nearly to the hospital already. Fear gripped Kay's heart. She'd been trying to think of nothing but getting to her sister's side. As the brown brick building came into view, her mind involuntarily began to process scary possibilities. Beth could be seriously injured. What if she had to stay in the hospital for days? Weeks?

There was no question that Kay would take care of the boys for as long as necessary. The question was *how* she'd do it. She was feeling like a failure after one evening. She couldn't feed Pete, couldn't figure out when his diaper needed to be changed. Will was up way past his bedtime and probably cried more in the last few hours than he ever did with Beth.

And what about Beth? What if she was left with a permanent disability? What if Rob had no life insurance? Kay didn't know anything about her sister's financial situation. Their family didn't talk about money.

"I'm just going to park in this lot so we can go in the emergency room." William's calm, practical voice filled the car and once again drove away the threatening emotions. "Surely someone in there can tell us where to find Beth."

Kay nodded. A strange detachment settled over her as her mind seemed to emphasize mundane things like the arrows on the signs and the way the parking lot had crisp, freshly painted lines. She sat motionless as the car stopped.

William reached over and touched her hand. It wasn't a caress or a squeeze, just a light tap that reminded Kay that he was there.

"Okay," she said. "Let's go." She pulled in a lungful of air as she yanked on the door handle.

Both babies had fallen asleep. William managed to unbuckle the older one and pull him into his arms without waking him. And it didn't take him any longer than it took Kay to figure out how to get Pete's infant seat detached from its base.

13

The emergency room shocked Kay with stillness. Fictional ERs were not set in rural Ohio. No one was running or pushing a gurney or yelling, "Stat!" There were four people in the waiting room, sitting as far from each other as possible. One of them coughed. A TV in the corner was playing a news channel. It was muted. Two women were behind a counter staring at computer monitors.

If it weren't for her racing heart, Kay might have felt as though she'd shown up early for some appointment. She walked up to the closer woman and opened her mouth.

The woman behind the counter spoke first. "Which baby is sick?"

"Neither," Kay said. "I'm, uh, my sister was in an accident. She should—"

"She'll help you with that." The woman nodded her head towards the other woman, cutting Kay off without even taking her eyes off the monitor.

Kay took a few steps to her left to place herself in front of the other woman behind the counter. She'd evidently heard – though her eyes also remained glued to the screen in front of her – because she said, "What's your sister's name?"

"Elizabeth Fisher."

The woman nodded, typed something, made a few mouse clicks, typed again. After what felt like a very long pause, her eyes finally moved from the monitor. They looked straight past Kay to the waiting room. "Have a seat over there," she said. "Someone will be out to update you shortly."

Kay turned and walked to the chairs, but she felt too restless to make use of one. She gently bounced her leg against Pete's car seat, hoping the movement would be similar enough to a car ride to keep him asleep. "Just a little longer," she whispered to him.

William didn't sit either. He shifted his weight slowly side to side. He was probably trying to keep Will asleep as well. The effort was unnecessary. The older baby was completely limp, his mouth hanging open, and appeared to be sleeping hard.

At five foot seven, Kay was not overly tall for a woman, which meant that William might be considered on the short side. He wasn't stocky or round. He didn't look short unless Kay was standing right next to him eye to eye as they were right then. And then he only seemed short if she thought about it. She was thinking of his eyes though. They were blue like Beth's.

Kay had thought her sister's brown hair and blue eye combination was rare when they were kids. Both of their parents had brown eyes to match their hair, just like Kay. Somehow she'd gotten it into her head that only blond people had blue eyes and she didn't pay enough attention to correct the assumption until at least her teen years. Beth had been an exception, special.

She was still special even if it had nothing to do with her eyes, and Kay still didn't notice a person's eye color until she'd spent a fair amount of time with him. That was where William was an exception. They'd met at work, only a few weeks after Kay finished college. She couldn't say what made her look so closely when he was introduced, but she immediately noticed the blue and brown combination she'd once thought rare.

She might have been gawking rather absently at him when he said, "Do you want me to try to find a bottle right away so we'll have it if, uh…" He gestured to the sleeping infant. "Or do you want me to stay with you."

"Stay," Kay said, which was kind of weird because she wanted him to go find a bottle. She was afraid Pete was going to wake up screaming, and she'd not be able to comfort him. The other people in the room would assume she was his mom and a terrible one. But she asked William to stay with her.

He didn't nod or say anything. He simply stayed.

They stood side by side in silence, swaying to different imaginary rhythms. The woman behind the counter must have had a loose definition of shortly because it seemed to take a very long time for anyone to come out to talk to them. Someone in scrubs appeared but approached someone else, then took that man down a hallway and out of sight. One of the women at the counter called out a name and made Kay jump. Someone else in the waiting room approached the counter.

Finally, a man in a white coat came through a door Kay hadn't noticed until it opened. He went up to the counter, and the woman behind it pointed at Kay. *At last*, she thought. The man in the white coat walked towards her. This was the person who would take her to Beth.

"I'm Dr. Everet," he said. "You're Elizabeth Fisher's family?"

"Her sister. Katherine Donovan."

The doctor nodded and held out a hand, not to shake but to point at the chairs behind Kay and William. "Have a seat," he said.

Kay just shook her head. There was no point sitting down if she was going to have to get up in a minute to see Beth. "How is she?" she asked, though she meant to ask *where* she was. Her brain and her mouth did not seem to be communicating properly.

"Well… she lost a lot of blood before she got here. We worked for a long time and did everything we could. Her injuries, however…" The doctor paused to draw in a long breath. "There was nothing we could do to save her. I'm very sorry."

A firm hand took Kay's elbow and guided her into the nearest chair. She set the car seat at her feet and noticed that Pete had started to squirm. She began to panic over the coming cry because that was easier than letting what the doctor said sink in. "I can't feed him," Kay said.

"Do you need someplace private to nurse?" Dr. Everet asked.

She shook her head, annoyed that he wasn't understanding her any better than she was understanding him. "No," she snapped. "*I* can't feed him. This is my sister's baby."

Pete let out a wail that echoed her frustration.

"Oh! I can help." The doctor looked pleased either for something to do or a reason to leave. He took off at a jog.

Kay leaned forward and unbuckled the infant's straps. She carefully pulled him from the seat and nestled him in her arms. She didn't rock or jiggle or try to offer words of comfort. She only held him. She didn't want him to be upset, yet she welcomed the cry that made thinking difficult.

Dr. Everet returned quickly and handed her a bottle of formula. It was warm. Kay's brain latched onto the temperature of the formula as the most important thing to think about. She ignored everyone except Pete. "Hey, little one. It's warm." She wiggled the nipple in his mouth. He didn't put up a fight. He sucked hungrily, hiccupping around the bottle as his cries subsided. "I didn't get it warm enough, did I? Was that the problem before? How do you think the doctor did that so fast? He wasn't gone long. I don't think it was a long time." Kay was desperately trying to picture an emergency stash of warm bottles somewhere in the hospital. She wanted to be amazed by the idea because she didn't want to think about anything else.

A stray thought pushed into her head, pushed aside her efforts to think only of warm bottles. It was a thought so scary she couldn't fully process it. But it was there all the same. The baby in her arms was an orphan.

~~~~

Kay Donovan woke up on the floor. Movement seemed to have woken her, footsteps. She opened her eyes and saw William stepping quietly around the room. He was picking up bits of plastic and dropping them into the large car seat box he'd opened the previous night.

"What time is it?" she whispered to him.

"After ten." He winced. "I didn't mean to wake you."

She waved off the apology as she sat up. "If it's after ten, I should be up." She rose only to sitting and looked around her apartment. There was a green tunnel probably eight feet long stretched nearly the length of her living room. Will popped out one end of it with a grin on his face before he turned around and crawled back in.

Pete was asleep in his new pink car seat. He wasn't buckled so he was slumped against one side. He didn't look particularly comfortable, but he looked asleep so Kay wasn't going to move him. There was a grocery bag on the kitchen table next to a box of Cheerios.

The Cheerios jogged her memory. Sometime around 5 AM, William had asked what they were going to feed Will for breakfast. Kay said she'd seen him eat Cheerios but didn't have any. Unconcerned with the early hour, William had called his sister Annie for advice as he left for the store again.

Will had opened his eyes while William was gone. Kay lay down next to him, hoping to keep him quiet and possibly disposed to sleep more. She had watched his eyes flutter closed but hadn't intended to go to sleep herself. She'd been only vaguely aware of William's return. Altogether, it'd been a very long night. The tunnel seemed to be the only thing her sleepy brain couldn't explain. "Where did that come from?"

"My house," William said.

That wasn't really an explanation.

William seemed to realize as much. He stopped tidying up and looked at Kay. "I stopped at home for a shower on my way to the store and thought... I bought that for my nieces at some point and thought it might entertain Will."

"At some point? How have I never noticed a giant lime green tunnel at your place?"

"It folds up."

"Oh. That's good to know." Kay pushed aside the blanket – she didn't remember taking it off her bed – and stood to stretch. Other bits of information began to come back to her. The sister she'd waved to so casually. The doctor who said he was sorry. The heart-rending phone call with her dad, who was going to handle everything when he got to town. She only needed to hold herself together until then. Kay tried to think practically about how to get through the next few hours. "It's Sunday," she said. "I need to go to church."

"You don't..." William appeared to consider what he wanted to say. "This is a difficult day, not a normal Sunday at all. I think God will understand if you can't make it to mass."

Kay glanced at the clock. There was a mass at eleven. She could make it if she hurried. "I need normal," she said.

"Okay. Will's been up about two hours. Pete's been asleep almost as long. He only drank half the last bottle. I... uh... I don't know if it's helpful to know any of that, but I guess... I'll watch them while you get ready."

"Thanks." Kay went into her bedroom and picked out a blue dress with white polka dots and took everything she'd wear with it into her bathroom. She showered quickly. She usually liked long showers to let her mind wander. There was no good place for her mind to go that Sunday. When the water shut off, she heard crying. She tried to dress quickly, but the lingering steam made her clothes stick to her. Then as the crying softened, she heard William's voice. He was trying to sing a lullaby but didn't know most of the words.

Kay stood with her hand on the doorknob and listened.

"Rock-a-bye, baby, in the treetop. Why is the baby in the treetop? I don't know the words to this song. But you stopped crying so I'm singing along. Rock-a-bye, baby, la la la la."

This was so far from normal. Kay wondered if anything would ever be normal again. Yet the moment wasn't as sad as it would have been without William. Did he plan to go to church with them, too? She was afraid to ask, afraid he'd say no. He'd need to leave eventually though. Kay was just going to continue getting through one minute at a time. Maybe her dad would arrive before William left. The babies needed her either way. She was not going to fall apart.

William looked up when she opened the door. He was holding a baby in each arm. Pete was lying across his left forearm and Will was held right-side up with the other arm. That meant William had no hands free to stop the older baby from grabbing his face. Will was tugging on his ear with one hand and trying to put his other fingers inside his nostrils. William was moving his head side to side to avoid such exploration. "Uh... I need some help," he said.

"Looks like you have everything under control."

"No, really, I'm stuck." William sent her a plaintive glance. "I picked them both up and now I can't figure out how to put either one down."

"Okay. Come here little guy." Kay scooped up Pete and held him against her shoulder. He immediately made a belching noise that explained the warm wet spot on the back of her dress.

"Oh, what did you do?" She pulled him away to look him in the eye when she asked the question even though she already knew the answer.

Pete grinned at her, a big toothless grin.

She couldn't hold back a small smile in response. "I see you at least feel bad about it."

He kept smiling at her.

"All right. Come with me while I change." Kay turned with the baby and laid him on the middle of her bed while she changed to a different blue dress with no polka dots. She was about to pick him up again when it occurred to her that the plain navy dress would be appropriate for a funeral.

Her hands froze right over her sister's child. Pete was so helpless, so innocent. His little legs kicked at the air while Kay blinked furiously to keep the tears from falling. It wasn't sad to return the dress to her closet, it was practical. She would likely need it in a few days. And she would need it to not be covered in spit-up.

The pink dress would work for church. She slipped her feet into a pair of sandals and grabbed Pete. She carried him out of the bedroom at arm's length to hunt down a dry cloth.

William was pacing with Will still in his arms. They looked surprisingly comfortable together, almost as though they hadn't been thrown together under the worst circumstances.

"All right." Kay flipped a rag onto her shoulder and held Pete there. It was the last dry one. "What do we need?"

William shrugged.

"I'm thinking out loud."

"I still don't know."

"Food, I guess. We must be almost out of diapers. Do we have enough to get through church?"

William stared for a moment, then said, "Are you talking to me now?"

"Yes."

"I bought diapers." He pointed to the shopping bag on the table. "But I don't know how many we need for church."

She nodded before walking to the table. She pulled out a package and tried to open it with one hand. Her fingers squeezed fruitlessly at the plastic. Then they slipped off and sent the diapers flying to the floor.

Will cracked up. William had enough sense to try to hide his chuckle.

Kay set Pete on the carpet near where the diapers landed and ripped into the package with both hands. Then she did the same to the larger size for Will and stuffed a few of each into the bag Beth had left with the babies. There were a few toys in there and a change of clothes for Will but not Pete. They'd already used up the infant's spare outfit.

"I guess Will should stay in his clothes from yesterday for now. I need to do laundry. I need more clothes for them both. And we need to go." She looked at the clock and wondered how Beth had ever gotten anywhere on time. She couldn't breathe. She opened her mouth and couldn't figure out how to breathe. She'd just thought of her sister in the past tense. It was impossible to do that and breathe at the same time.

3

$\mathcal{K}$ay had been on the verge of tears at least a dozen times since William had arrived with car seats. He knew she couldn't fight it forever. She really had lost her best friend. Crying would be healthy and natural. She might even need to cry. That was why William felt like the worst kind of person for hoping each time that she'd mange to wait a little longer. It was going to be so hard to watch.

It was hard to watch her be miserable and know there was absolutely nothing he could do to fix it. It was about to happen anyway. Kay was crouched by the diaper bag gasping while her eyes turned red. Tears were finally inevitable.

He stepped closer and held out his free hand. Kay took it. She pulled herself up and buried her face in his shoulder as the flood began. It was a loud cry. Will stared at her with a startled expression. William bounced him gently and tried to offer a reassuring smile.

Kay continued to cry and Will continued to look at her as though she'd turned into an alien. William held them both, one hand jiggling the baby and the other patting Kay's back. They'd all make it if he only had to stand there to be supportive. If anyone was looking for words of comfort or wisdom, well, that might be the end of his composure, too.

Then Pete joined in with a sudden and heartfelt wail. Rather than compounding the situation, his cry jolted Kay into action. She pushed away from William with a deliberately calming breath. She grabbed a few tissues and wiped her face. The tissues stayed crumpled in her hand as she picked up Pete again.

"Back to business," she said. Her chin jutted out stubbornly as though she'd let herself be distracted by something trivial. "So we need…" Kay's voice trailed off as she seemed to be making a mental list. She glanced at William uncertainly before her eyes cleared with the arrival of a new thought. "You still have the car seats in your car, don't you?" she asked.

He nodded.

"We don't have time to…"

"I'm coming with you anyway. I'll drive."

Kay asked him to go ahead and get Will buckled so William took the little guy out to his car and put him in the back seat. Pulling the straps in place, he realized how loose they were. Had he driven to the hospital and back without noticing the baby wasn't properly restrained? How had he been so stupid? William palmed his face, which made Will giggle. William smiled back and went to work securing the straps, trying to push aside the guilt over what couldn't be changed. He simply said a quiet prayer that Will hadn't been harmed and that Kay hadn't noticed his incompetent help.

She appeared on the stairs with Pete and a diaper bag, then disappeared into her apartment again. She didn't come all the way out before she went back inside with the door open behind her. Finally, she came out and locked the door. She hurried down the stairs. William realized too late that she didn't have a free hand to open the car door. She shifted the diaper bag up to her shoulder to open the door before he made it to her side of the car.

He jogged back around to start the car and the air conditioning. Summer was waning, but it was still summer.

They walked into church as the opening hymn ended, which was actually not as late as William thought they would be. Both babies were awake when they sat down, an open pew in the second to last row. Everything went well for a good ten minutes. Then Pete started to get fussy. Kay reached into the diaper bag and pulled out a bottle of water and a bottle of powdered formula. It would be a lot easier for her to mix them with both hands free.

William had one arm around Will as he knelt on the pew next to him. He took Pete with his free hand while Kay prepared a bottle. When she was ready, she tried to take Pete back. But Will had climbed nearly on top of him trying to get on William's lap. Kay set the bottle between them and grabbed Will so William could offer Pete the bottle. Will found an interesting button on the front of Kay's dress, and there was another minute of peace.

But hunger didn't seem to be Pete's problem. He had barely begun sucking on the bottle when he arched his back and turned away from it. He appeared to be working himself up to a very impressive volume. William stood quickly to make his way out of the sanctuary. When Will realized that William was leaving, he shrieked to go after him.

The four of them ended up sitting in the gathering space listening to the mass over speakers that might have been installed for such a situation. Both babies fell asleep shortly before the congregation began to file past them. William was thinking that he could go for a nap, too. He wasn't in a hurry to stand up or to leave.

He heard Kay sigh heavily next to him before she said, "I have two babies now."

There was something disbelieving in her tone that went beyond the moment. William had been curious about her plan, whether or not she intended to keep the babies. He didn't want to ask if she wasn't ready to think about it. Just because she said it didn't mean she was ready to think about it. He still didn't ask. He only turned to her and waited to see if she had more to say.

"Beth asked me... Several months ago, when she was pregnant with Pete, she said she and Rob needed to make a will and would it be okay if they listed me as the guardian for their children? Of course I said yes. I was flattered. I had this beautiful picture in my head where I got married and asked Beth the same thing and we raised our kids together knowing that we were each other's backup plan."

Kay started crying again as she spoke. It was a calmer cry, tears dripped down her face as though she didn't even notice them. "It wasn't supposed to be like this. I don't know what to do now. I mean, I can't go to work tomorrow. I don't know when I can go to work, but I can't just quit because obviously I need money so I guess I need to figure out some sort of day care situation but I don't know how to do that or if... I don't even..."

"Excuse me, are you okay, honey?" An older woman, probably at least seventy, had apparently noticed Kay's distress and stopped in front of her.

Kay nodded and hastily wiped the back of her hand over her face.

The woman opened her mouth. Her eyes flickered between Kay and William as she thought about what to say.

William felt Kay shrink against him. She hated small talk under normal circumstances. "Thank you for your concern," he said. "There's nothing you can do though. She, uh, she recently lost her sister."

"I'm so sorry." The older woman put her hand over her heart. "What was her name?"

"Beth." Kay barely whispered the name.

The woman had sharp ears. She nodded and said, "I'll add Beth and your family to my prayer list." Her eyes washed over the two adults and two sleeping babies and took them as a family.

Kay said, "Thank you," to the woman's back as she moved away. Then she finished drying her face as she cast a wary eye to the other stragglers, those who stopped to talk on their way out of the church. Though she moved slowly to avoid waking Pete, her intent to leave was clear as she gathered her things.

Will's eyes flickered open when William shifted to get to his feet. He didn't fully wake though. He stayed limp and breathed heavily. William followed Kay from the building and was reminded of when he used to follow her out of work for a chance to talk to her.

They'd both started working at Timmond's right out of college. That had been a year later for Kay so William was fairly settled there when Kay became the new girl. She was there only a few days when some coworkers started talking about how odd it was that she refused invitations to join the others in the back room during breaks. William preferred a few quiet minutes at his desk to listening to inane chatter, but chose the former only occasionally to avoid being labeled the weirdo loner. He admired Kay for having the guts to be by herself.

Kay shared an office with William and two other women. The others quickly began sharing smirks whenever Kay was on the phone. They'd noticed that she seemed to draw in a steadying breath before each call. They thought it was funny that she thought talking to customers was difficult. William never laughed because what he'd noticed was that she thought it was difficult and did it anyway. How could that not get his attention?

Of course her looks hadn't hurt. The long brown hair got his attention. The shy smile got his attention. The way she walked got his attention. The office generally cleared out at five o'clock on the dot so timing his exit to coincide with hers was not much of a challenge. The challenge was getting her to share more than a few words before she reached her car. But they were some of his favorite words of the day.

William eventually worked up the courage to ask for some real time together. It's possible there had been a picture in the back of his mind of the two of them someday taking kids to church. The current situation was nothing like that picture. Kay buckled Pete before she climbed into the front seat with a stoic look on her face. William couldn't tell if she was lost in thought or simply trying not to think about anything.

He started the car and just sat there. He wasn't sure if he should take her straight home or if she'd want to stop somewhere first. He'd gotten maybe an hour of sleep so his brain wasn't fully functional and his tongue was tied by a fear that anything he said might make her start crying again.

"So if you were me…" Kay stopped, wrinkled her face in thought and then started again. "I can't decide how to tell Matt. I'm not sure even this situation justifies bothering my boss at home, but I hate to blindside him first thing in the morning with the news that I'm not coming in for… well, probably a few weeks if he'll let me. What would you do if you were me?"

"Let me think." William considered both what he would do and what he thought would make Kay most comfortable. He knew that part of her just didn't want to have a conversation with her boss about her personal life. "I guess I'd send him an email today to explain the situation and give him a heads-up that you'll call in the morning to discuss details. That way you don't have to say what happened out loud and maybe he'll… you can both go straight to time off and practical stuff."

Kay nodded. She didn't look remotely comfortable with the thought.

"So, uh…" William glanced at the back seat. Both car seats faced the back so he couldn't see either baby with their seats in the way. He wondered how long they would stay quiet. "Do we need anything before I take you home?"

Kay closed her eyes as though fighting off physical pain.

More tears. It was unavoidable and not entirely his fault, but he still felt responsible for saying the wrong thing.

Her eyes opened and they were red but not watery. "I hate this," she said. "I hate this so much, but I think we have to go to my sister's house."

William felt his eyes widen. He hadn't expected that at all.

Kay reacted defensively. "The boys need things. Their things. Cribs mostly. We can't all sleep on the floor every night and it doesn't make sense to buy new ones when they have cribs at… And they need clothes and more bottles and Will's high chair and… I have to do what's best for them even though it's hard. Maybe having their own things will make my place more comfortable for them. More familiar."

William nodded along with everything she said. She hadn't gotten that much more sleep than he had and was likely still in shock over the loss, yet she was thinking far more rationally than he was. She really was amazing. "You're right," he said. "Do you have a key?"

"Yeah. I've never used it. Beth just gave it to me to hold in case she ever locked herself out, but… I think I… let's just go."

William put the car in drive and followed Kay's directions. He'd talked to Beth and Rob a few times but didn't know them well. It felt incredibly intrusive to walk into their house. He was sure, however, that his unease was nothing compared to what Kay must be feeling.

31

"How can I help?" he asked. He was ready to do anything to get this over with.

Kay looked around as though she expected someone to come around a corner and startle her. Her breathing sounded erratic. "Can you keep an eye on the boys while I gather things?"

"Okay."

She gently placed Pete on the living room carpet. He immediately started crying. She walked away without a look back. William felt that she either trusted him to handle it or was as determined as he was to do this task quickly. Even with the fussy baby, he knew he'd been given the easier share.

Kay walked in and out several times with pieces of a crib she'd dismantled. She stacked the parts against the wall, enough for two cribs. Then she set a big box of baby clothes next to them. Then William realized that they had a huge problem. His car wasn't nearly huge enough to hold all the things they needed to move.

He searched his tired brain for people he knew with trucks. He worked with a guy who had a pickup. Chris was pretty easygoing. He'd probably let them borrow the truck, or drive a load for them. And William even had his number. He pulled out his phone. Luckily, the babies were fascinated by the glowing screen and stared quietly at it while he talked.

Kay returned to the room while he was explaining the dilemma to Chris. She had a grocery bag in each hand and baby blankets draped over her shoulder. She put everything down slowly as she listened. Then a look of utter incredulity washed over her face. She, too, was kicking herself for not realizing sooner that cribs wouldn't fit in his trunk. She stood there and waited for him to finish the call.

It seemed likely that Kay figured out the plan from his side of the conversation. William explained anyway. "That was Chris, from work. He's happy to help, but he has some errands to run himself. He's going to come over here to swap vehicles, then he'll meet us at your place in an hour or so."

Kay tipped her head to the side as though waiting for more.

William watched her hair swing out from behind her back. Why was she looking like she was expecting something else? Chris would bring the truck. They'd load up the stuff. It wouldn't take an hour to... Oh. He palmed his face again. Even when he thought he was helping, he wasn't helping. "We can't take the babies in the truck."

Kay nodded at him. She didn't appear frustrated that he'd bungled the plan. She just stood there waiting to hear how he was going to fix it.

"All right. I guess one of us needs to go ahead and drive the truckload to your apartment. I hope you'll let me do that so you don't have to lug all that up the stairs." She was wearing a dress. Surely she'd see it made sense for him to do the physical part. "That won't take an hour so I'll meet Chris back here and we'll all take my car back to organize your place as soon as he returns it."

"Here." She took a few steps and reached into the diaper bag. "Take my keys now so I don't forget to give them to you."

William took the keys with what sounded like permission to do the heavy lifting. Somehow, he still felt that no matter what he did, he was giving Kay the more difficult job. After he explained his mistake to Chris, who stuck around long enough to help him load the truck, he left Kay at her sister's house with two fussy babies and what might be a million painful memories.

He left everything inside the door of her apartment rather than guess where she wanted it. Though William wanted to rush back, he stopped at a fast food place for some burgers. Kay hadn't eaten yet that day and he was hungry, too. They'd just finished

33

eating when Chris returned to reclaim his truck. Kay was ready to leave. William helped her get the babies in his car as soon as he had his keys.

But then she ran back up to the house, leaving him wondering what they forgot. She was inside for several minutes so he started up the car to keep it cool inside for the little ones. He stood waiting on the passenger side, making faces at the boys through the window. They rewarded his efforts with big smiles.

Kay didn't appear to be carrying anything when she arrived at the car. He didn't intend to pry, figuring she just wanted a minute alone. But she explained anyway. She pulled a small necklace from her pocket. It had half of a heart dangling from the chain. "Beth and I have had these since we were little. They're kind of juvenile so neither of us wears them anymore, but I wanted to put Beth's with mine. I don't know why. I just know that... that I don't ever want to come back here." Her voice broke and she could barely get out the last few words before her head fell onto his shoulder. Her arms hung loose while she just leaned on him and cried.

William tentatively put one arm around her to pat her back. His fingers stroked her silky hair. He reached around with the other hand and gently pulled her closer. He hated how insufficient his support felt. And he hated himself for thinking it felt wonderful to hold her when she was hurting so much.

"Your dad will be here in just a few hours," he said.

It didn't seem to help. Her head barely moved in response.

"You'll get through this. I don't know how, but I know you will."

Her head moved a little more. He wasn't sure if she was nodding or drying tears on his shirt. She really did feel good in his arms. He didn't know how he was going to get through it either.

4

The arrival of Kay's dad, Patrick Donovan, lifted a bit of her stress. She stopped worrying about questions she couldn't answer as he took charge of answering them. He worked with Rob's parents to make funeral arrangements and hired a lawyer to address guardianship and estate issues. He emptied their house and got it on the market, though a lot of its contents were simply put into storage to deal with later.

Kay's new life was pretty well organized by the time he returned to Seattle. While she appreciated his help and would certainly miss him, she also felt a little relieved when he left. He seemed to be channeling all his own grief into anger and spent much of his two-week visit yelling at people to get things done.

He took the constant tension home with him. He also took Sherry with him, his wife. Sherry was technically Kay's stepmom, but she never thought of her that way. It wasn't that she wouldn't think of her like that. She had just never known Sherry in a motherly role. Kay and Beth's mom died when they were in college. Kay was in her first year and Beth in her third. Their dad married Sherry a year later, at which point they were already planning the move to Seattle. They'd been married more than four years now, but the distance kept Kay from getting to know Sherry in any role.

Her dad had booked an early flight on a Tuesday. The hotel was near the airport so Kay had an awkward goodbye with Sherry Monday night, then a goodbye with her dad that started sweet and turned even more awkward. He apologized for being cranky, broke down in tears, then turned and punched the doorway on his way out. Kay closed her apartment door with a complete lack of emotion. Her heart was demanding a break. There was nothing safe enough to feel.

She went through the motions of getting the boys ready for bed. She'd gotten surprisingly good at juggling them in the two weeks they'd been living with her. There wasn't even a hint of satisfaction as she thought about her progress. She cradled Pete in one arm while she helped Will into his pajamas. She asked him to lie on his back so she could hold down the toe of the footies with her knee and zip them one-handed.

She checked Pete's diaper. They'd both been changed recently and still seemed dry. "Okay." She tried to reward Will for his cooperation with a bright smile. It didn't feel bright on the inside. He smiled back though. "Let's go to the bedroom."

Will stood up. He'd taken a few steps during the last week and she thought he might try again. After a few seconds, he dropped to all fours and crawled, presumably because it was faster, into the bedroom. Kay followed him. She had a double bed, which was pushed into a corner of the room. Two cribs were lined up against the wall by the foot of her bed, and there was just enough space to walk between them. Or crawl. Will used the leg of his crib to pull himself up and stood waiting. He already knew Pete would get tucked in first.

Kay swayed on the spot for a moment before she placed Pete on his blanket, then wrapped him up nice and snug like a baby burrito. Then she leaned over to pick up Will, who stretched his arms towards her as she reached for him. She held him close as he snuggled his head against her shoulder. She wondered briefly if she reminded him of his mom or if he'd already forgotten Beth.

She closed her eyes, patted his back, and began to sing. When Kay tried to establish a bedtime routine, she didn't know if it would be better to sing a lullaby or say a prayer. She wanted to teach them to say a nighttime prayer, but they were a little young for that. On the other hand, she didn't know any lullabies. She settled on singing the Our Father to them. She sang slowly and softly, placing Will on his back in the crib as a long amen fell from her lips.

He quickly flipped over and stuck his tiny butt up in the air, his preferred sleeping position. Kay stepped to the side and checked on Pete. Sometimes she had to sway longer and put him down several times before he was ready to go to sleep. His little eyelids floated up and down though. He looked ready. She watched until they stayed closed.

Then she got herself ready for bed and tucked herself in. It was not a restful night. Pete woke her up five times instead of the typical two or three. Will had been sleeping through the night but was an early riser, generally wanting out of the crib close to 6 AM. She thought Pete was fussing again when the clock said 4:22. It was Will. He seemed wide awake and under the impression that 4:30 now qualified as morning.

That weird numbness was still clinging to Kay, and she didn't even feel annoyed with Will for getting her up so early. She simply scooped him out of his crib so he wouldn't wake Pete.

Pete joined them before long anyway. Kay muddled her way through another day. Maybe because of the early start and maybe because she was just really lucky that they napped at the same time, Kay was able to get a shower before noon.

The freeze on her emotions began to thaw as 5 o'clock approached. She was giving Pete a bottle while she rolled a ball around on the floor with Will. "Do you think William is going to stop by today?"

Will mostly ignored the question as he chased the ball, but there was a hint of recognition on his face. Did he hear the difference between Will and William or did he just think she was talking to him? "It's Tuesday though," Kay said, mostly thinking out loud. "He always has dinner with his sister's family on Tuesdays."

William lived only a half mile from Kay, and her apartment was on his way home from work. Since he helped her move the baby stuff, he'd made a habit of stopping every day when he passed, checking in to see if she needed anything. He'd stayed only a few minutes whenever her dad and Sherry were there. And today he'd have only a few minutes before going to Annie's house. In fact, Kay's apartment was not on the way if he was going directly to Annie's house after work. Hope shifted to disappointment. "We might not see William at all today."

Will gave an unexpected squeal of pleasure as the ball slipped from his fingers and bopped against a wall.

Kay laughed at his amusement. "I guess we can have fun without him," she said. "And if he comes tomorrow, maybe we can talk him into staying for dinner. I think he likes to be fed about as much as the two of you."

When the bottle emptied, Kay switched Pete's position to try to pat a burp out of him. She'd talked herself out of expecting William so she was startled when the doorbell rang. Will crawled to the front door before she could even get to her feet. Of course, he didn't have far to go.

"Hi." William greeted her with a smile while his eyes flickered gingerly over Kay and the babies.

She understood his caution. Showing up at her place had been a rather unpredictable mess lately. Once she'd opened the door crying. Once she'd handed him a smelly baby before he even said hi, before *she* even said hi. Once her dad answered the door yelling about inconsiderate salesmen before he recognized William. It was something like a miracle that he kept coming back.

"I thought I was making myself pretty predictable," William said. "You almost look as though you've never seen me before."

Kay felt oddly flustered as she backed up to let him in. How had William ended up as such a good friend to her when their relationship began with an awful date? She wasn't about to ask him that. "I just... um, it's Tuesday. Aren't you going to Annie's for dinner?"

"Yeah. As a matter of fact, that's one of the reasons I'm here. Hi, kiddo." He lifted Will into his arms as he spoke because the baby was reaching for him.

"This isn't on the way. How is it one of the reasons you're here?"

"Uh... well... Annie sort of invited you and the babies to dinner, too."

"Oh." Kay had stood and chatted with Annie after church several times. That didn't qualify as knowing Annie. She didn't have the energy for tense socializing. "I don't think I'm up for being around people tonight. It was nice of her though."

William opened his mouth and stuck his tongue out at Will, which made the baby giggle, before he addressed Kay again. "So... uh, maybe invited isn't exactly the right word."

"She didn't invite me?" Embarrassment heated Kay's face for refusing an offer she hadn't actually received. She should have asked him to clarify instead of assuming that sort of invited was the same as invited.

William was a little distracted by Will trying to grab his face, but there was clearly something else making him uncomfortable. Finally, he said, "It was more a threat than an invitation. She told

41

me that I had to bring… had to figure out a way to convince you to come because if I showed up without you she would refuse to feed me."

No wonder he looked uncomfortable. He knew she wouldn't want to come, but if she didn't he would suffer for it. Maybe. Kay didn't know Annie nearly well enough to know if the threat would have follow-through.

"Please," William said. His eyes chased the word with a plaintive look.

"Why does your sister even want a stranger and two babies as dinner guests?" Pete echoed her question with a loud burp, as though trying to prove her argument. He was so little that everything he did was impossibly cute though. She wasn't sure if it proved anything.

"Annie loves babies. She also thinks you need support and that I am apparently chopped liver. I think she has this idea that she's going to become your mentor or something." William squinted doubtfully at her as he paused. He seemed to realize he wasn't convincing Kay to come with him and was thinking of what else to say. It appeared he was going to be pushy, which wasn't like him.

She guessed that meant he was expecting follow-through.

"She'll want to hold Pete a lot," William said. "That'll give your arms a break. And she's a pretty good cook."

Kay felt her refusal evaporating. She knew she didn't have the energy to spend an evening coming up with chitchat. She just wasn't sure she had the energy to keep shooting down William's offer either. He could have run away when her world turned upside-down. But he jumped right into the somersault with her. It took a lot of strength to disappoint him, especially when she was a little confused by the way he sounded as though he was trying to do yet another favor at the same time. "Okay," she said on a sigh.

"Okay? You're... coming?"

"Let me grab a few things." She turned to check her diaper bag. Pete had just eaten, but it wasn't smart to leave home with no formula. And she'd need at least one dry rag for whatever didn't stay in his stomach. Plus diapers. It wasn't called a diaper bag for nothing.

They took separate cars, which Kay said was so he could go straight home afterwards. It was really so she could leave without him if he seemed to want to stay longer than she did. Of course, she knew he knew the real reason. There was an odd satisfaction that came with knowing she didn't fool him.

Annie and her husband Jake lived on a weird little dead-end street lined with houses and surrounded by farmland. They had a large yard with a swing set and various outdoor toys strewn about. Kay pulled into the driveway behind William, who made it to the back of her car the same time she did. He unbuckled Will while she grabbed the diaper bag and Pete's carrier. She walked slowly to let William reach the door first.

"Hey! Come on in." Jake answered the door and opened it wide. "So this must be Will," he said as William entered.

Will stared at Jake and his grip on William's shirt tightened.

Kay followed them inside far enough to let Jake close the door.

Annie came rushing towards her with her arms out like she was going to hug her but dropped her arms at the last moment and said, "I'm so glad you came. How are you feeling today?"

"Um... better." That was probably the best simple answer Kay could give. She wasn't fine. She was a long way from fine. But that day at least, she didn't feel as though she was being crushed by sorrow and that was better than a lot of recent days.

Annie nodded and looked into the baby carrier. "Pete, right?"

"Yeah."

"I want to hold him so bad. Do you think he'll let me? Will you let me?"

"I'll get him out," Kay said. It was plain that Annie wasn't exaggerating. Her desire to hold the baby radiated off her. Kay undid his straps and passed him to Annie, then shoved the carrier and diaper bag into a corner.

Annie beamed down at Pete while her girls gathered around her oohing and ahhing and asking to see him better. She squatted to show off the baby.

Kay felt vulnerable without a baby to draw attention away from her. Jake was looking at her as though thinking of something to say. Kay swallowed and tried to dive into small talk. "How old are your girls again?" she asked.

"Bailey is seven." He pointed at the tallest girl. She had skinny legs sticking out of her shorts and light brown hair in a messy ponytail. "Then Ariana is five and Taylor is two." The middle child had thin but wavy hair nearly to her waist and the youngest smiled sweetly when she heard her name.

"So… Ariana just started kindergarten?" Kay asked.

Jake nodded. "This is her second week."

"Can I hold him?"

"No, I want to!"

"I get to hold him first!"

The older girls had started fighting for a turn with Pete, and Annie looked up from the growing chaos. "Do you mind if I sit them on the couch to hold him for a bit?"

Kay shook her head. Annie had a lot more experience with babies than she did. It wouldn't make any sense to second guess her judgment. She followed Pete and his new fan club into the next room where Annie lined the girls up on a couch to pass the baby between them. He started fussing during Ariana's turn and Taylor scrambled off the couch. She had no interest in being near someone making so much noise. Annie scooped Pete into her arms and calmly shushed him.

"Come with me into the kitchen," Annie said to Kay. "I think dinner's almost ready and I'm going to have to give him back in order to get the casserole out of the oven."

Kay trailed after her with a look over her shoulder at William. He was still standing by the front door with Jake talking about something sports related.

Though he'd seemed engrossed and didn't look her way as she left the room, William stepped into the kitchen only a minute after Kay. "What's cooking, Annie?" he asked.

"Dinner," was her curt response.

William made a frustrated face, but it was exaggerated and clearly intended only to amuse Will.

Annie picked up on the fake annoyance and rewarded him with more information. "It's a macaroni casserole, with beans and tomatoes. Plenty of cheese."

"Smells good."

"I'm afraid it's done," Annie said. "That means I have to give you up for a while." She was talking to Pete, whom she passed to Kay before opening the oven.

Annie pulled her husband into the kitchen to help insert a leaf in the table, then grabbed a high chair from a corner and pulled it closer. They'd just gotten a booster for their youngest so Will ate in the high chair. Kay held one baby during the meal while William fed the other. The food was good, and someone else had cooked. Kay was actually fairly relaxed. Then the questions began.

"How long are you able to be off work?" Jake asked.

"I'm not exactly sure." Kay took a breath and tried to explain without too much detail. "Matt... uh, my boss said I could have twelve weeks family leave. But it's unpaid. I'm using up my two weeks of vacation first and I don't know if I'm going back twelve weeks after the two weeks or including the two weeks because I'm not sure my savings will last that long. I think it will. But I've never budgeted for diapers and formula before. Matt's expecting to hear from me halfway through or so… probably early October, to establish a restart date." She stuffed a forkful in her mouth to shut herself up. That had been too much detail. She babbled when she was nervous.

Jake was nodding as though his question had been answered though. Mostly. "Forgive me if I'm prying, but your sister didn't have insurance?"

Kay shook her head while she forced the food down her throat. "My dad is taking care of all the estate stuff, but it doesn't… He said they had no insurance and were upside-down on their mortgage and… I'm not expecting anything there."

"But you found someone to watch the boys while you're at work?" Annie asked.

"Sherry has a niece… Sherry is, uh… sort of my… she's my dad's wife. And she has a niece in the area who runs a day care from her home. One of the kids she was watching just started kindergarten."

"I'm in kindergarten," Ariana said, her eyes glowing with pride.

"Yes, you are." Jake nodded at his daughter.

Kay felt attention shift back to her. It seemed she was expected to say more. "Anyway, since they no longer need full time care, that kid's parents aren't going to use her anymore and Sherry's niece said she could fit both Pete and Will. She's holding the spot until I need it."

"Does she live near you?" Annie was looking at Pete, but Kay could tell she wasn't asking him.

"Closer to work," she said.

"Good." Annie looked up at Kay. "It sounds like the practical things are falling into place. We'll be able to help with other things, advice and social support. We're really glad you agreed to start joining us every week."

"Oh, yeah," Jake said. "Annie needs this weekly baby fix so she doesn't start thinking we need another one." He shot his wife a playful wink.

She waved it away. "We're doing it for Kay. Trust me," she said, locking eyes on Kay, "there will be times you'll be looking forward to Tuesday just to talk to someone who talks back so you won't think you're going crazy."

Kay nodded stiffly and broke the eye contact to silently ask William why these people were under the impression that she'd made a commitment that extended to all future Tuesdays.

William was asking Will if he wanted more to eat when the baby had plenty of food on his tray. His fake oblivious act telegraphed guilt. The man had a sneaky side. Perhaps he didn't fully deserve the hero status she'd been building up for him in her head. He would pay for this transgression.

5

William Dakley walked up the stairs to Kay's apartment the following Tuesday expecting a fight, or at least a battle of wills. He'd seen her every day since the meal with Annie and Jake. Some days he stayed only long enough to be assured that she didn't need anything. She had let him stay for dinner once though, and they'd spent Saturday afternoon together. They'd simply watched a movie and played some cards. It was a lot like the Saturdays they'd spent together before there were two babies in the picture. Except that there were two babies in the picture. The movie had to be paused twice, the cards were interrupted by a diaper change, and they both played part of the game trying to keep Will from grabbing the cards.

William had invited himself to sit with Kay and the boys during church on Sunday. They all went out for lunch afterwards. It was something else they used to do. Kay's life had changed radically, yet she still seemed to have a place for William. But at no point in all the time they spent together during the week had either of them mentioned the fact that Annie and Jake were expecting both of them on Tuesday.

He reached the landing with the familiar white railing and blue siding and pressed the doorbell. A baby was crying inside. Pete was his guess. It might have been his imagination, but it seemed that the infant's lungs had strengthened quite a bit in the last few weeks.

Kay opened the door and thrust Pete into his arms. "You try," she said.

Oh, good, William thought. *She's already agitated. That will make this so much easier.* Then he squelched the internal sarcasm in case the baby could sense it. "What's going on, little one?" He spoke softly to Pete, who probably couldn't hear him over his own wailing. He tried to bounce gently as he closed the door behind himself.

"His naps have been short today," Kay said. "I think he's tired but won't go to sleep."

"Maybe a little ride would help." William studied Kay as he made the suggestion. She clearly picked up on the hint. She only shrugged in response.

William knew that she knew he'd tried to trick her into committing to the regular dinners at his sister's house. He also knew that didn't mean she was committed. And that she was seriously upset with him over the whole thing. The fact that she was so blatantly waiting for him to be the one to bring it up unnerved him something awful. It might be a heated conversation. He didn't want to have it over a screaming baby. Getting Pete calm would have to be the first step.

He walked the length of the short apartment to provide some motion. Unfortunately, that didn't help, and it made Will aware of his presence. The older baby toddled over and grabbed William's leg, cutting off the possibility of more ineffectual pacing. He looked down at Will. "Hey, buddy. You're really getting the hang of the walking, aren't you?"

This observation was meant as a compliment, and any rational person would have taken it as such. Will burst into tears. William froze. He'd just walked in and already he felt over-whelmed. How did Kay do it?

She came over and tried to pick up Will. His little fists clenched so tightly on William's pant leg that they pulled a few of the hairs underneath. Kay didn't force him to let go. She just took Pete instead with a nod towards Will. "He wants you."

She did not say, "You are so useless." She probably wasn't thinking it either. But William would not have blamed her if she was. Not only had he failed to comfort the smaller baby like she'd asked, but his arrival had set off the older one. Some help.

He bent to pick up Will. The curly-haired toddler had moved from screaming to smiling before William had straightened again. Pete was still crying. Was anyone – other than perhaps Will – grateful the status quo had been reestablished?

Kay's body language didn't say she was grateful. She didn't sway with Pete but switched her weight jerkily from side to side. Her shoulders were tense and her eyes a little crazed. Yet she held Pete to her shoulder, where he could scream right in her ear, and responded to his cries with soothing words. The woman was a model of self-control. Even with red eyes and a spot on her shirt, she was a beautiful model of self-control. William watched her as he sat with Will and tried to get the baby interested in the toy he'd been playing with when he arrived.

Eventually, Will was happily sorting shapes and Pete's cries faded to whimpers. Kay whispered, "Is he asleep?" Then turned her back so William could see the tiny face over her shoulder.

The infant's eyes were closed, and he let out a sigh bigger than he was.

"Looks like it."

Kay took a calming breath. She continued to sway though, not taking any chances.

Into the quiet, William ventured to ask if Kay had started anything for dinner.

"I barely had lunch," she said.

She was hungry. That could be good or bad. It could make her more receptive to letting Annie do the cooking. Or it could make her cranky and more stubborn about the whole thing. William decided to be a man and take the plunge. "Annie and Jake are expecting to feed all of us tonight."

"Yeah, I gathered that."

"We'll need to leave soon to be on time."

Kay almost smiled. "If you're concerned about being on time, you didn't need to stop here first."

"They're expecting both of us."

"*You* told them I was coming. *You* can tell them you were delusional when you said that."

"Hopeful," William corrected. "I was hopeful when I said you'd come every week because I was hopeful that you'd want to. I am very sorry about the way I went about this though. I admit it was underhanded of me. I just thought that… You enjoyed yourself last week, didn't you?"

"Your sister is a good cook." Kay said this as though she'd just thought of it, as though it had nothing to do with what they were discussing.

"Are you coming with me or not?"

"Not."

William had gotten frustrated with dancing around the topic and now regretted making the choice so simple. He tried to backtrack. "I think you would like going over there if you give yourself a few weeks to get used to it."

"I think I would like for someone to tell me when going somewhere raises the expectation that I'll be going there regularly."

"You like doing things regularly."

"I like choosing what things to do regularly." She stopped

swaying and Pete picked his head up briefly. Kay patted his back and moved side to side as he settled back into his nap. Her whole demeanor softened. "I'm mad because you told them I was coming every week and now it'll look like I'm backing out."

"I said I was sorry. And it won't look like you're backing out if you come."

She glared at him, which was actually a good thing. It meant she was thinking. There was a chance she was thinking about coming.

William tried to think of his sister's good qualities but stopped himself before he began to list them out loud. That would feel too much like matchmaking, even though he sort of was matchmaking. Annie's best friend from school had moved away several years ago. She still talked to her on the phone but hadn't really connected with anyone locally. And Kay needed a friend, not a replacement for her sister but someone who could patch up some of the hole. He was sure Annie and Kay could become close.

Plus, there was Jake. William liked the idea of him and Kay spending time with a couple. Maybe that would help her see that they made a good couple, too. They made a good couple most of the time anyway. When Kay wasn't being unreasonable. "Look, I knew you'd be uncomfortable at first, but if you were forced to spend more time with Annie and Jake, you'd start to consider them friends."

"You tricked me for my own good?" She cocked her head and used her free hand to pull her long hair away from Pete's growing spot of drool. "Is that seriously the stance you want to take?"

He had tricked her for her own good, but for his own good he wasn't going to say it that way. "I'm just trying to help."

Kay widened her eyes expectantly, as though she expected to

hear exactly how he thought he was helping so she could explain exactly how he was wrong.

William was not wrong. He happily met the challenge. "It's a free meal once a week that someone else cooks for you. You've admitted cooking with babies can be rough."

"Getting out of the house with babies is no picnic either."

"That's why I'm here to pick you up."

"*You* could cook for me *here* if you really wanted to help."

She'd gone back to being unreasonable. They both knew he was a terrible cook. "I set off the smoke detector again a few days ago. Don't think it'd be helpful to do that here."

"You're not incapable," she said. "You just don't want to learn."

She was pretty even when she was rolling her eyes at him. William tried to focus on reasons they should go to his sister's house partly to put the brakes on reasons he'd like to be alone with Kay instead. "Annie *likes* to cook for people," he said. "It's almost like doing her a favor. And she has three kids. Regular get-togethers will be a chance to casually ask about any day-to-day kid-wrangling that might come up."

"You think I can't do this on my own?" There was a sad mix of defiance and doubt in her eyes.

"Of course you can, but why try when there is someone who can help you? Even if you never have questions, she might just become your go-to babysitter. Don't you think there might come a time you'd like to leave the house without the kids?"

Kay stared at him, apparently at a loss for an answer.

William turned away as something hard banged against his arm. Will was hitting him with a plastic square. His babbling seemed to be a request for William to take a turn putting one into the box. William pretended to think about it before dropping the shape into the box. When he returned his eyes to Kay, she was not pretending to think. She was really stuck. Her mouth hung partially open as she tried to figure out what to say.

It occurred to William that she may have thought *he* was going to be her go-to babysitter. That idea made him picture sitting right there watching these babies while he watched her leave with some other guy. It was a thought so disturbing he wished he hadn't brought up babysitting at all. But why didn't she just say that she didn't need anyone else to watch the kids? Didn't she trust him enough? Sure, the smoke detector at his place got a regular workout, but he'd never actually set anything on fire.

The silence between them stretched on while Will kept passing plastic pieces to William. Finally, Kay pushed aside her strange expression with a forced laugh. "Does your sister know you're signing her up for babysitting and advice and such or is this like how I thought I was agreeing to one dinner?"

"Please. Did you not have to pry the baby out of her hands last week? You won't have to ask her to babysit. She'll offer."

Kay closed her eyes with a sigh. "I need a clean shirt," she said.

That was as close to, "I'm going to come because you're so right about everything," that William was going to get. He jumped up to take Pete while she changed. He didn't even care that he hadn't convinced her. He knew she had only agreed because she was too tired to argue. He also knew that another week with Annie and Jake would make her feel more committed to the routine. It would be much easier to talk her into coming next week. And someday, if she and Annie became friends, she might even admit it had been a good idea to trick her.

Annie did her part. She welcomed Kay casually as though she'd already been coming regularly. Then she relieved her of the baby a minute after she'd walked in, trying to give Kay's arms a break. She certainly wasn't snubbing Will. Annie had tried to take the older baby first, but Will was old enough to care who was holding him, and he clung fiercely to William.

It filled William with a strange sort of pride to have the little guy so attached to him. It wasn't as though he'd done anything to earn the affection. He'd simply been around enough to be familiar. He gave the boy a return squeeze though, assuring him that he wouldn't be set down until he was ready.

Will was ready soon after they'd all gathered in the living room. He seemed less intimidated by the girls and wanted a closer look at the game they were setting up on the floor.

Annie exclaimed in delight as he started to move across the floor. "Oh! He's walking!"

"Aw," Bailey said. She held her arms out to encourage him to keep toddling towards her.

"Had he taken any steps when he was here last week?"

Kay looked at Annie. She looked a little guilty about something. "Yeah," she said slowly. "He'd taken a few steps on and off. But he's only really gotten the hang of it in the last few days. I feel awful that I don't remember exactly which day he took the first step."

"Oh, phooey." Annie dismissed the guilt with a wave of her hand. "He's right around fourteen months, right? No one will expect you to remember anything more specific than fourteen months."

"How old was I when I learned to walk?" Bailey asked.

"Thirteen months."

"What about me?" Ariana looked between her parents.

Annie smiled. "You were about fourteen months, just like Will."

The five-year-old beamed at the baby, even though he'd begun to grab pieces of the game.

William eased himself to the floor and tried to guide Will to the dolls Taylor was playing with instead.

Taylor scooped up both the dolls and yelled, "My babies!"

"Taylor, you have two babies. You can keep one and give one to Will." Annie spoke softly yet firmly.

Taylor clutched the dolls more tightly to her chest.

Will wasn't interested in the dolls anyway. With William on the floor, he jumped onto his lap and pushed his little hands against his shoulders. William knew what he wanted so he turned away from the couch to have room to fall backwards and pretend Will had pushed him over.

The toddler squealed with laughter and someone – William couldn't tell if it was Bailey or Ariana from his vulnerable position – yelled, "Get him!" He had just enough time to brace himself before all three girls were on top of him, too. Plus two dolls, one of which caught a hard plastic foot on his ear. "This is comfortable," he mumbled.

Much laughter met the comment. William spent the next several minutes acting as though he couldn't get out from under the pile of kids, which prompted a whole lot more laughing.

Fortunately, Annie called the girls to dinner before he had to prove he was acting. William pulled himself off the floor after the pummeling feeling suddenly older than twenty-five. "Your girls are stronger than they look," he said to Jake.

Jake nodded with a commiserating smile. He'd been buried under those girls a few times himself.

Kay smiled at both of them. It was fleeting but nice to see. At least one of her smiles during dinner didn't look strained. William was sure it was healthy for her to get out of the house even if she only did it because she was too tired to argue.

She was tired though. They returned to the living room after they ate and had been chatting only a few minutes when William saw her head tip sideways against the couch. Her eyes closed, and she was out like a light.

Jake noticed and quieted the room by taking the girls outside to enjoy the still bright summer evening. Their excited screams came through the walls as happy background noise. Will was sitting on the carpet with one of the dolls he'd not been allowed near earlier. He wasn't exactly playing with it. He was picking at the hair with a funny look on his face. It kind of looked as though he was trying to figure out why anyone would want to touch that hair even as he kept touching it.

Annie had Pete on her lap and was making her face do all sorts of weird things to get him to smile at her. It must have been working because she'd been at it since she sat down.

William smiled a bit himself at his sister's expression and at Will's. But he couldn't quite relax. Obviously, Kay needed the sleep. He was still uneasy about letting her. He whispered to Annie as he nodded at Kay. "She's going to be embarrassed when she realizes we've all been watching her sleep." He didn't want her to feel embarrassed, and he didn't need another reason for her to be annoyed with him.

Annie eased up on the exaggerated faces so she could whisper back. "No one's watching her, and we understand. When Ariana was a baby, I fell asleep in the dentist's chair." She turned Pete to tuck him into the crook of her arm as she stood and jerked her head towards the kitchen. "Still," she said, "if you think it'll make her feel better, we can be more obvious about not watching."

Annie led the way from the room and William motioned Will to come, too. The little boy stayed on all fours to keep up. His hands made tiny slapping sounds across the hard floor of the kitchen. They went through it to a room clearly intended as a formal dining room. Annie called it the quiet room. There were a couple of beanbag chairs and a squat bookcase whose shelves were filled with books going up and down, across, sideways, and every seemingly impossible angle. A child-sized table sat in a corner covered with art supplies and half-finished pictures.

Will didn't stop as he entered the room. He crawled directly to the bookshelf and began tugging out the books on the lower shelf. William pulled a squishy green chair close enough to intervene if he moved his attention to the upper shelf. Upsetting that balance might cause an avalanche of books on his little head.

Annie remained standing, swaying with the infant. Her attention focused on William and Will. She smiled faintly, but there was something sad in her expression.

"What?" William asked, not entirely sure he wanted to know what she was thinking.

She took a deep breath. "Now don't take this the wrong way."

He rolled his eyes at her. "Oh, this is gonna be good. When your sister starts with, 'Don't take this the wrong way,' there's definitely an insult coming."

"No, there's not. I just... I..." Annie narrowed her eyes in thought. "I want to say I'm sorry without sounding like I'm sorry about... I mean..." She sort of glanced between the babies.

"There's *no* way to take that because it doesn't make any sense."

"What I mean is... well, you seem very... I think you've become attached to these babies already."

"And that's a bad thing?"

She shook her head. "I'm kind of impressed, if you want to know the truth. A lot of guys would be seriously put off if a woman they were chasing was suddenly saddled with raising someone else's kids. You didn't bat an eye."

William felt she had no reason to be impressed. Everything had happened so fast. He hadn't had time to bat an eye. He hadn't made any decisions. Undeserved or not though, what she said sounded an awful lot like a compliment. It probably wasn't what she worried he'd take the wrong way. "What's your point?" he asked.

"What I'm trying to say is that I'm sorry for what you're going through, and I don't want to sound like I'm saying I'm sorry these precious babies are in the picture... only about the circumstances that put them in the picture."

"Tell Kay."

"I have. I hope I've been clear on that at least. She absolutely has my sympathy, but I want you to know you do, too."

"Save it for Kay." William picked up one of the books Will had tossed on the floor to distance himself from his sister's mushy words. "I don't need your sympathy. I'm not the one grieving."

"Maybe not, but—"

"Save it," William snapped. He hadn't realized he was getting angry. "I'm fine."

"You're not fine."

"Yes, I am." William's words had a clear edge to them. He was afraid that proved his sister's point. That made him angrier, which really meant he wasn't fine. "Compared to Kay, I'm fine," he added.

"People have survived wars, you know."

Great. Now he was angry and confused. It was a good thing she'd warned him not to take the conversation the wrong way.

"People have watched while their relatives were tortured and killed," Annie said. "People have lived through atrocities we can hardly imagine."

"What does that have to do with anything?"

"*That's* my point."

"What is?"

"Don't compare yourself to anyone else. Others have suffered worse than Kay and that doesn't invalidate her suffering any more than her situation means you're not allowed to feel bad and I'm not allowed to feel sorry for you."

Her speech sounded very motherly. William already had a mother. He didn't need another one who was only seven years older. He opened his mouth to tell her to shut hers.

"I'm not finished," she said first.

That sounded so much like the mother they shared that his mouth snapped shut on instinct.

"I remember when Jake's dad died. I know how hard it is to watch someone you love suffer a loss. It doesn't take anything away from Kay to admit it's hard on you, too. That's all I want." She paused and sighed as though she couldn't believe how difficult he was making things. "I want you to admit you have feelings. Just say, 'Yes, it's hard. Thanks.' And then we can move on."

William glared at his sister while he regurgitated the words she wanted. He was even more ready to move on than she was. But for some reason, a heap more words came spilling out before he could stop them. "It's awful. She cries all the time and I feel like a world class jerk for wishing she'd stop crying. And she's not a hugger. Two years we've been friends and she never touched me. Then all of a sudden she keeps throwing herself at me. Every time I'm afraid I might not be hugging her in a strictly friendly way and she'll figure something out and the last thing I want to do is scare her away when she's trying to lean on me. I'm trying to help as much as I can, but half the time I think I'm just getting in the way and… I blame you. I blame you for everything."

Annie burst out laughing then threw a hand over her mouth as she glanced back towards the living room. She looked a lot more worried about waking up Kay than about offending the person she was laughing at. "That's quite a speech. You blame me for all that?"

He tamped down the laugh trying to join hers. He actually felt better for having gotten a few things off his chest. There was no reason to let his sister think she deserved any credit. "You are the one who told me to back off and try being her friend."

"I said for a while. You're the one defining a while as… years."

William only sort of growled a response. He wasn't defining anything. Kay was a hard person to get close to. He was waiting for her to define it.

"And I stand by everything I said," Annie added.

He remembered exactly what she'd said. He also remembered that he hadn't meant to spill his guts that day either. He'd been talking about Kay at Tuesday dinners since she started working with him. That he couldn't help. And he mentioned when she'd agreed to go out with him because that felt like news. When he'd showed up the Tuesday after the date intending to keep all the awkwardness to himself, Annie was very persistent. She got him to admit the date was horrible. It was tense and full of painful silences and he was sure Kay didn't want to be there at all. She'd probably only said yes to try to be nice.

Annie insisted it wasn't hopeless. She said a woman didn't need to be immediately attracted to a man, that she could become attracted over time if she realized he had qualities she respected. Like dependability or faithfulness or common goals. William didn't really think Annie's advice would work, but he had little choice in following it. He'd promised Kay that things wouldn't be weird at work no matter what so he had to be friendly. And he was still interested in her so he had to keep trying even after he changed jobs.

Annie wasn't particularly concerned about defending her old advice though. Pete had gotten fussy, and she'd turned him around to face her. She was talking to the baby as though they were the only two people in the room.

Will was looking at the books he'd thrown off the shelf, most of them board books. He handed one to William, who took it and waited for the toddler to crawl into his lap. He opened the book and began to read. Will crawled back down three pages in. He handed William a different book. That one held his interest only long enough for William to find the first page. He crawled up and down with a few more books before Kay stepped uncertainly into the room.

"Hi," she said.

"Hi," William said. He looked up at Kay. Her hand was on her face trying to cover a red line from the side of the couch that didn't make her any less beautiful. The distraction earned him a board book to the groin. He winced before he invited Will to come up and look at another page or two.

"Thanks again for bringing the babies," Annie said. "We are getting along so well." She didn't break off her eye contact with Pete even though she was talking to Kay.

"Yeah, um… It's about time for his next bottle, a little after actually, and I was thinking I should take him home first so I can put him to bed right after."

"Oh, sure. Whatever's best for the little guy." Annie looked more disappointed than she sounded.

"I mean, if you're ready to go." Kay was talking to William. He'd ridden with her.

"Of course," he said. "Come on, Will. Let's find all your stuff." He stood and scooped Will into his arms. They hadn't gotten out much so it was easy to grab the diaper bag while Kay got Pete buckled into his carrier. She looked perkier than when he'd arrived to pick her up. Surely after a delicious meal and a nap she was ready to forgive the guy who tricked her into coming, not that he was going to bring it up in front of Annie.

They said their farewells and stepped outside.

Jake was trying to teach the girls kickball. It wasn't clear how much they were learning. He rolled the ball to Ariana, who tried to kick it and missed. Jake looked over to William and Kay as she chased it, with Taylor on her heels. "You guys heading out?"

"Yeah," William called. "Thanks for everything."

Jake waved and said, "See you next week."

Kay waved back, then turned and shot William a dirty look. Maybe he wasn't completely forgiven yet. He wouldn't bring it up when they were alone either.

6

"Did you hear about Timmond's?"

William looked up from his work. "What about Timmond's?"

"They're closing." Chris sat on the edge of the desk, clearly delighted to be the one to share the gossip. "Apparently, they got a call from corporate this afternoon saying their branch is being shut down as of 5 o'clock today."

"They're closing *today*?" William couldn't believe it. If Timmond's closed, Kay would have no job to go back to.

"Yep." Chris nodded with relish. "Everyone got two weeks' severance and a sorry about your luck. You used to work there, right?"

William only nodded.

"Bet you're glad you jumped ship." Chris didn't wait for an answer before he chased a passing coworker. "Hey, did you hear about Timmond's?"

The other coworker nodded and the two of them walked away with their heads together discussing the big news. Timmond's was a competitor so the closing might mean more business.

William sat there with no idea what he'd been doing when Chris interrupted. Kay did not deserve another blow like this. No one did. But Kay was the only one on his mind. She'd been doing well. It'd been a few weeks since he'd seen her with red-rimmed eyes. Despite being constant reminders of Beth, her children were helping Kay move through the grief.

She'd really bonded with the babies. She took them to their 4-month and 15-month well visits and came back reporting that they'd both gained weight. She said that was proof she was doing something right. And she'd even been referring to herself as their mom. William had no doubt she loved them like her own.

She'd also stopped giving him a hard time about the weekly dinners with his sister and even seemed to look forward to them. She admitted she liked the adult company and forgave William enough that she invited him to stay for dinner somewhat regularly when he checked in after work.

He wanted to call her to see if she knew what her employer had done to her. But what good would that do? He couldn't offer much comfort over the phone. What if somehow she hadn't been told yet? What if Chris was spreading a false rumor? He didn't think Chris would do that on purpose, but William hadn't asked where he'd gotten the information. He could be mistaken.

William flipped his computer to the Timmond's site. He clicked on the list of branch offices. Sandusky was still listed. It felt like false hope. He couldn't quite dismiss it though, not even when his entire office was buzzing with the news.

It was past four already. William moved a few papers on his desk looking for something to do. It was going to be impossible to concentrate, but he only had to try for a little while. Then he would clock out and talk to Kay. He tried not to look at the time at all, which of course meant he looked at it constantly. Eventually, though it couldn't have gone any slower, time passed and William left work.

Kay's house looked as cheerful as ever as he parked in front of it. She rented from an older couple who lived downstairs. They marked the passage of time with ever-changing decorations. The beach balls and strings of shells had been taken down at the start of September, replaced by a wreath of fall-colored leaves and cornstalks. Now, at the middle of October, two pumpkins had been added. Kay had been looking forward to Halloween. She said the boys were too young for trick-or-treating but that she'd like to dress them up, put them in the stroller, and walk around the neighborhood listening to people say how cute they were.

He knew as soon as she opened the door that she wasn't thinking about anything so frivolous. Her eyes were red and her face splotchy. There had definitely been a lot of crying. William didn't think he had any real hope that the rumor was false, but he felt enough disappointment to prove something had been alive.

Kay turned without a greeting and motioned him to follow her inside. Pete was lying on a blanket looking up at a toy with several dangling things. Will was working on a wooden puzzle. Kay sat between them, probably returning to where she'd been when he knocked. She shook the strings above Pete. He smiled and tried to grab them. She smiled back at him, but her eyes looked totally defeated.

William sat next to her without saying anything either. Will hit him in the kneecap with a puzzle piece he was trying to hand him. William took it and slipped it into the right place in the puzzle. Will grabbed the little red knob and pulled it back out. He handed it to William again.

"I guess, um, I guess you got some bad news today."

Kay shrugged and kept her eyes on Pete.

If he didn't know her better, William might have thought she was blowing off his concern. But he did know her. He'd seen that shrug before. It meant her thoughts were swirling too fast to put into words. He tried to help Will with the puzzle while he waited.

The toddler didn't seem to want help putting it together. He just wanted to pass the pieces back and forth while he figured it out himself.

William sat on the carpet feeling very much in the way yet again.

~~~~

Kay's head had been a jumbled mess all afternoon. She had longed for William to arrive so she could tell him everything. Maybe he'd see a solution that she didn't. Now that he was there, she didn't know where to start. Everything was wrong, and everything was probably going to get worse.

"Rob's parents were here today," Kay said. "They brought new toys." She supposed that was a small bright spot. Both babies had been a little easier to entertain with interestingly new items to put in front of them.

William nodded.

"They're gonna be so upset if I have to take the boys to Seattle."

William's head froze in the middle of a nod. "Seattle?"

"I don't know." Her dad had reminded her that coming to live with him was an option. Since she considered that her last resort, she maybe shouldn't have said it first.

"Is that... a possibility?" William stared at her. He looked angry.

She really shouldn't have started with Seattle. "You know my dad invited me and Will and Pete to live with him and Sherry."

"You said you'd never want to do that."

"I don't *want* to," she said. "You heard about Timmond's?"

"Yes. Matt called you?"

"I have no job." Kay wasn't particularly fond of the job she'd lost. After being home with these boys for weeks, she hated the idea of going back to it. But she'd accepted that it was necessary. "Matt apologized up and down, but it's not his fault and he's out of a job, too."

"They're really shutting down the branch?"

Kay nodded. She knew she should be more upset about the job, but it felt like the least of her problems. "I... have no childcare either."

"What happened?" William looked as though he had a million more questions. His jaw was set as though he was forcing all the others to stay inside.

"Amanda called me. That's Sherry's niece. Amanda White. She called a couple days ago and..." Kay paused and hoped William wasn't angry that she hadn't told him sooner. She was no good at sharing bad news and embarrassed that she hadn't fought harder for the boys. Even though she didn't think it would have made a difference. "And... well, she asked if I still wanted her to watch Pete and Will. I said yes, that I was scheduled to start back the Monday after Thanksgiving. She said she'd found a family who needed her right away and if I couldn't start paying her right away, she'd rather take their kids."

"I thought she was holding a place for you." William sounded indignant when he interrupted.

Kay wasn't sure if he was indignant at her or on her behalf. She folded in a little. "I did, too. But I didn't actually talk to her when Sherry arranged everything so I don't know exactly what was said and, well, if she needs the money sooner that's something I can understand. She's..." Kay shrugged off the memory of what had been a very awkward conversation. She wanted to kick herself for not just calling Matt to say she'd come back sooner but obviously

71

that would not have worked out well either. "I thought I had a few weeks to find something else. I didn't know what the options were and now I know I don't have many."

"So now Seattle is an option?"

Why did it sound like he was yelling at her for not knowing what to do? "I don't know," she said again. "I don't know *yet*. I'm trying to figure this out. There aren't many day care centers in the area, at least that I can find. Most are in someone's home, and I don't know how to tell if I can trust someone with the babies and mostly everything is more expensive than Amanda was. I think maybe Sherry talked her into a better deal and she was looking for a way to get out of that or... Anyway, I found a church-run preschool that has day care and I thought I could actually afford it before I realized they don't take infants so I couldn't use them until Pete turns one and that doesn't do me any good before June and there are some subsidies I might be able to apply for except that now I don't even know what my income is until I find a new job but how can I look for a job if I have nowhere to leave the babies?"

"I'm sorry," William said. "I thought... freaking out isn't helpful. How can I help?"

Kay tried to accept the apology with a smile. She hoped he couldn't see the effort it took. It wasn't his fault that every time he apologized it reminded her of the first time, the time he said he was sorry he asked her out. She knew she'd been tense and closed off the whole date. She knew she wasn't making a good impression. But there was no off switch for nerves. William made her *very* nervous back then.

She'd had a big crush on him. Her face got hot enough to burn holes in whatever thoughts she was trying to have when he was near. The confidence didn't help. His confidence, not hers. She knew he'd been at Timmond's less time than most of her coworkers and yet he seemed like the most capable person in the building, the one most people went to with questions. It was difficult not to find that intimidating.

She wasn't sure how she'd even agreed to go out with him. Apparently yes took less courage than no. She couldn't squash the nerves when they were alone and hoped he'd give her a second chance to relax. He hadn't. He might have said something like, "Should we try this again?" Instead, he said, "This was a bad idea. I'm sorry I asked." And that sounded a lot like, "I can't believe I thought I was interested in you."

When William told Kay he wouldn't make things weird at work, she assumed he was going to help her avoid him. It was a surprise to have him continue to come up to her desk to say hello and follow her out at the end of most days for a quick chat. She didn't know if it was pity or a need to prove he wasn't scary. Since scary was not the same as intimidating, either reason was insulting. The only good thing was that it fairly effectively eliminated any swoony feelings she'd had. The man was relentless though.

Eventually, she got so used to him that she forgot to be insulted. Eventually, she let her guard down and realized he was just genuinely being nice. He was only sorry he tried to put a romantic spin on the relationship when they were fine as friends. The timing worked well. They'd only seen each other outside of work a few times when William confided that he was being poached and would not work at Timmond's much longer.

The two of them had spent most Saturdays together since he'd changed jobs and finally felt like true friends and not just friendly coworkers. And now, when Kay desperately needed a friend, William was coming over nearly every day. He was amazing, and she was treating him in a way that made him want to apologize. Some friend she was. "*I'm* the one who should be sorry," Kay said.

"*I'm* the one who's freaking out. I didn't mean to sound like I was yelling at you."

"You were yelling at me, but I deserved it."

"Ba ba ba ba." Will was waving his hands excitedly over the finished puzzle.

"Hey! Good job, Will."

He smiled and started pulling the pieces out one by one.

"Do you know what he was trying to say?" William asked.

Kay only shrugged. "He's doing a lot of babbling and sometimes I think he's trying to say actual words but I haven't clearly identified any yet."

"No Mama?"

"Not yet." She looked at Will and at Pete, whose little legs were kicking the floor next to her, and another wave of uncertainty washed over her. "I hope it's okay."

"What is?"

"Me having them call me Mama." She wanted to explain, to get William's opinion. "I was getting Pete into a bath a few weeks ago, and I thought about how I was referring to myself in the third person. It's hard not to talk to them even though they can't talk back and there usually isn't... I mostly just narrate the day. Aunt Kay's gonna do this and Aunt Kay has to get that and... and it occurred to me that for all intents and purposes I'm going to be Mom to these guys. I haven't yet, but eventually I'll officially adopt them and... Anyway, when I thought that, I just... out of the blue... I had this memory of Beth. I remember Beth saying... We were still in college and we were watching this thing on TV about orphans in, um, I think it was somewhere in South America... Beth said, 'I think every child should be able to call someone Mom.'"

William nodded at her. He seemed to be agreeing but she wasn't finished.

"But she didn't have kids yet when she said that. What if she… I'm not going to pretend that… I haven't figured out the best place, but I want to have a picture of Rob and Beth where the boys will see it regularly so they'll know they were their parents first. And Beth was Mommy so I'm using Mama."

"That's a good idea. Both the picture and the different version of Mom." William glanced around the apartment as though he was wondering where the picture could go. "And I'm sure it's fine for you to… they should be able to call you Mom. Or Mama." William's voice got a bit deeper when he was serious.

Kay wasn't very good at eye contact anyway. Hearing the bass tones made her eyes land on his mouth, which made her imagine him kissing her, which was a very unexpected thought. She turned quickly back to Pete to get it out of her head.

"So, uh, what are you thinking?"

Did he know? She was still thinking about William trying to kiss her. She was thinking how much she'd like to let him.

"Are you thinking job first or day care first?" he asked.

Right. Kay had far more serious problems than some wayward thoughts. "I think I know what I need to do. I'm just not happy about it."

William stayed silent. When she looked at him, he widened his eyes to prompt her.

"Everything was lined up so I could enjoy being home with the boys another month, but now… I think I need to find a job that starts as soon as possible. If I can get income sooner – with the severance, which is two weeks' pay I wasn't counting on before – I can begin a job before my savings is completely gone. That would give me a cushion to take almost any day care situation at least until I can, hopefully, figure out what's affordable long term."

"Okay." William let out a long breath as though everything was settled.

"This is assuming I can convince someone to hire me soon."

"Okay," he said again. "I'll help you look. Annie and Jake can help, too."

1

Annie and Jake did want to help, though not as much as William tried to impose on them. The now regular Tuesday dinner was four days after Kay lost her job. She was feeling somewhat proud of herself for having already sent her résumé to several places, some more promising than others. Only one company had responded so far, but they'd asked for an interview. Annie said she would be happy to watch Will and Pete during the interview. That's when William opened his big fat mouth.

"Why didn't I think of this before?" he said. "Annie can watch the boys."

"I just said I would."

"No, I don't just mean during the interview." William looked across the table at Kay. "You don't need day care at all. You can leave the boys with Annie while you're at work."

Kay had joined them for dinner often enough that she'd gotten reasonably comfortable around Annie and Jake. When William volunteered his sister for a full-time, unpaid job on her behalf, her comfort level dropped right under the table. Where she wanted to kick William's shin. Hard. The only thing that stopped her was how still the room had gotten. Someone would notice the kick. What if they thought it was only for asking at the wrong time?

"That was his idea," she blurted. That didn't mean she hadn't agreed to it. "I mean, I wouldn't ask you to..." She didn't ask. William did. Kay was too flustered to be clear.

The kids had now caught up with the conversation, too. "Oh, you mean the babies would be here every day?" Bailey's eyes lit up. "That would be great. We can watch them."

"Yeah," Ariana said. "I wanna play with them every day."

"You'd be at school most of the time," Annie said. That pretty much killed the girls' enthusiasm.

William was looking a bit sheepish. Kay didn't know if he'd figured out on his own that his suggestion was out of line or if he'd felt the mental kick.

"I know that's too much to ask," Kay said to Annie without quite looking at her. "Don't worry. Just pretend no one said anything."

"Let me be blunt." Annie smiled kindly through her bluntness. "I couldn't let you pay me to watch the boys. I just wouldn't feel right about a situation where I felt like I was working for a friend. And watching them full-time for free... well, I probably would start to feel taken advantage of. So that's not going to work." She glanced at her brother then back to Kay so quickly it looked as though she was rolling her eyes at him. She may have been rolling her eyes at him. "However, while it's a bad idea long term, I could definitely help out temporarily. I can keep them for a week or two if you have any trouble getting start times to line up. Or just occasionally, if you have to work weird hours or one of them is too sick for day care. Within limits, I have your back and am happy to help."

"Thank you," Kay said. She felt a little less frazzled. Annie was so clear about her limits that Kay believed those were her actual limits and not just her trying to be nice because William opened a can of worms.

"Good," Jake said. He looked ready to change the subject, which would also help tamp down the lid on that can. "I passed a help wanted sign on my way to work this morning, and I was going to stop on the way home to get some information to see if that might be something that would be a possible fit for you but… I forgot." He made a face that said he was annoyed with himself. "I'll check in the next few days though and let you know what I find out."

"Thank you, too," Kay said.

"Do you have a deadline?" Jake asked. "Or a backup plan if you can't find something by the deadline?"

"Thanksgiving." Kay squirmed at the unfortunate timing. It was going to be difficult to be thankful if she didn't make that deadline. "I mentioned that my dad offered to let me and Pete and Will move in with him and, uh, Sherry if I have to. If I don't have income by Thanksgiving, I think I'll have to take him up on the offer. I'll need to get out before I have to pay December's rent."

"Would you run into any penalty for breaking a lease or anything?" Jake asked.

"No. No, I don't have anything formal with my landlord. I just pay them on the first of each month."

Jake nodded and stuffed a huge bite into his mouth. It seemed unlikely that he had any more immediate questions.

Kay tried to get in a few bites herself while the pressure was off.

"Sherry is your stepmom?" Annie had questions. The tilt of her eyebrows suggested this wasn't the simple yes or no it sounded like, but a leading question.

Kay chewed faster and nodded while she swallowed.

"Do you, um, do you have trouble getting along with her?"

"Not yet," Kay said. "I don't really know her. My dad didn't marry her until I was out of the house. So I worry about trying to get to know her while sharing living space. What if we have different ideas about cleanliness or how the kitchen should be kept and I might need to feed these little ones at odd times and I just know their house isn't babyproof. It'll be hard to live there without moving things around and that could get awkward. It would have to be temporary. I could only stay with them until I could save enough for my own place and that puts me in pretty much exactly the situation I'm in now only on the other side of the country. I mean, I've never even visited Seattle. I'd do almost anything to not have to move there but…" She gestured rather helplessly to Pete, who had been asleep on the floor. He woke as she was talking and began to fuss.

She got up to retrieve him. She had to do whatever it took to care for her new babies, even if it meant eating one-handed. Even if it meant moving three time zones away to a thoroughly foreign city.

William met her eyes as she returned to the table. "Don't worry," he said. "You'll get a job here, and you won't have to move."

She didn't believe him when he said, "Don't worry," because he looked very worried. She just nodded and sat Pete on her lap. He was very grabby so she gave him the spoon while she ate with the fork.

After dinner, the girls talked their parents into starting *It's the Great Pumpkin, Charlie Brown*. Jake groaned because they'd apparently watched it three times already that year. Kay hadn't seen it since she was a kid though, and she was kind of talked out from all the questions at dinner. The show sounded like a nice break.

William said he was going to help Annie clean up the kitchen. He took Will with him though. He probably wasn't going to be much help with a baby in his hands.

~~~~

Annie eyed her brother suspiciously. "If you really want to help, I can hold Will."

"You can try," he said.

"Come here, big guy." Annie held her arms out to him.

Will smiled at her, but he leaned closer to William at the same time. He wasn't scared of Annie. He seemed to understand that he was being given a choice and was showing his preference to stay with William.

Annie sighed and put her arms down.

William smiled at his sister, even though he knew it was juvenile to let a baby drive a popularity contest between them.

"Poor kid," Annie said as she began putting things in the dishwasher. "You've brainwashed him."

"Yep." He grinned at Will, who grinned back as though they were sharing an inside joke as he bounced. William moved his arm to bounce him faster like he wanted. Will giggled and William kept bouncing him while he talked to his sister. "I really just followed you in here to say I'm sorry I tried to sign you up as a free day care center. I wasn't really thinking."

"That's usually the case."

"Very funny."

Annie dumped out a pan that had been soaking and straightened her expression. "Well, I forgive you. Kay seemed more upset by your lack of thought than I was though."

"I know. And I think she's only just forgiven me for tricking her into—" He cut himself off before he created another problem.

"What did you trick her into?"

"I guess I've been panicking a little since Kay's been talking about moving to Seattle."

She pressed her lips together for a second, letting him know she noticed the subject change but wasn't going to chase it. "She didn't sound very happy about it either."

"Exactly," William said. "She *wants* to stay here so it isn't entirely selfish of me to want her to stay here."

"She said she'd do 'almost anything.'" Annie turned to face her brother as though she was expecting a response.

"I heard. What's your point?"

"That might give you an opportunity."

"What opportunity?"

"You could ask her to marry you."

"That's ridiculous. We're not even dating."

Will suddenly got tired of the bouncing and squirmed to be put down. William complied and watched him toddle quickly – it was almost a run – into the living room. He intended to actually help with the dishes now that his hands were free but was distracted by the fact that Annie was looking highly amused about something. "What?"

His question caused her to smile bigger. "That is interesting."

"What is?"

"You said it was ridiculous because you're not dating, not because it was a bad idea or because… it almost sounded like you already thought about it."

He was nuts about Kay and that wasn't a secret. At least it wasn't a secret from Annie and he assumed she told Jake. It wasn't a secret. That the idea of marrying her had crossed his mind wasn't a huge leap. Nor should it amuse anyone. "That's not interesting," he said flatly.

"If she doesn't have a job in a few weeks, she might be desperate enough to say yes."

"And that's not funny."

Annie's expression sobered. "You know, I might not be entirely kidding. You're going over there every day to help with the babies and you two seem to get along really well. Being married might not be all that different."

William did see Kay every day, but he went home every night. "It would be a lot different."

"You would go there." The way her eyes darted around said she'd picked up on the suggestion.

"It's the main thing that separates marriage from other relationships," he said. "It's pretty important."

Annie nodded to concede his point, but then she said, "Kay seems to like you. She might not mind so much."

"Yeah, I want to marry someone who doesn't mind so much."

He wasn't sure if Annie laughed at his sarcasm or at her own teasing. "I guess you better start by asking her out."

"You better stop trying to help me."

"Hey." She gestured to a messy counter. "I'm helping more than you are."

"Debatable," he said. But he grabbed a rag to wipe down the counter anyway.

8

This was it. Maybe. This could be it. It could be the day things started looking up. And it could be a truly awful day. William shut off his car and faced Kay's house. The downstairs door still sported a bright red and yellow wreath of leaves. The cornstalks and pumpkins were gone though. A row of turkeys wearing pilgrim hats now paraded by the front window. Thanksgiving was two days away.

He was dying to know if Kay had gotten the call and yet he didn't want to know. Everything hinged on that phone call. She'd been on several interviews but had gotten no offers. Her last interview had been the previous Thursday. She'd enlisted William's help with her backup plan all weekend. They looked at routes to Seattle, researched hotels, guessed how long she might be able to drive in a day with two babies, priced rental trucks. Over and over, she said she hoped they were doing the research for nothing.

Over and over, he asked why she couldn't get a loan from her dad. She said it was because he offered to let her move in, he hadn't offered money. She couldn't turn down a generous offer with a request for a different one. William thought there might be something beyond manners that stopped her so he quit pushing the idea.

Now everything came down to whether or not she'd been offered that job. She was told to expect a decision on Monday. She heard nothing on Monday. She promised to call if no one called her on Tuesday. If she didn't get the job, she would spend Thanksgiving with him and Annie and her family – instead of the usual Tuesday dinner – then drive away Friday morning.

She had to stay. William got out of his car and walked up her steps. He knocked on the door. He'd convinced himself she was about to open it to share the good news when she opened it and said absolutely nothing.

"Hi," he said.

"Hello." She shivered at the cold air rushing through the door. "Come in and close that."

He did as she asked. The apartment seemed smaller than usual, which didn't surprise him. He was carrying enough apprehension to fill a palace.

Kay walked a few steps to her kitchen table and glanced at the phone sitting on top of it before she turned back. "Do you want to stay for dinner?"

He stumbled over a nod because he was expecting news, not a simple question. Was she watching her phone because she still hadn't heard about the job?

Will grabbed him around the legs and said, "Up, up, up."

William bent to pick up the kid. "How are you today?"

The toddler pushed away to be put back down. It was just as well. As much as he liked the little guy, it was Kay he wanted to talk to right then. "Still no answer?" he asked.

Kay looked up from her phone. She gave her head a quick shake, looking sad and distracted.

Anger welled up inside William. How could this company leave Kay hanging for so long? They'd said she'd know on Monday and now she didn't know on Tuesday. And why hadn't she called them like she said she would?

"Will!" Kay moved quickly to redirect the toddler, who was trying to climb on a box.

The real reason the apartment seemed smaller smacked William in the face. There were several boxes in the room, a stack of books that wasn't usually there, stuff on the counter that should be tucked away in cupboards. She had pulled things out to start packing. "Are you packing?"

"I have to."

"You're assuming the delay means no?"

She wrinkled her eyes at him in confusion, only for a moment before they flitted back to her phone, then to each of the babies.

A little of the anger William was trying to keep in check found its way to Kay. "Shouldn't you call them first?"

"What?" She looked startled. "I told you I didn't get the job."

No, she hadn't. He was confused at how she thought she'd told him something she hadn't, but the news itself shook right through the confusion. He didn't want to believe it. "You've started packing?"

She didn't respond. She just glanced at her phone again, and it wasn't even on. That wasn't what made him snap though. It was her resignation. She looked so calm, like she didn't care at all about leaving him behind. "Kay! What is so fascinating about that phone!?"

Out of the corner of his eye, he saw Pete flinch right before he started crying. Will ran to Kay, also in tears. William felt like a monster for scaring the boys. "I'm sorry," he said to the room at large. "I'm really sorry." He deliberately worked to calm himself, at least on the outside.

Those few soft words were all it took to settle Will. He appeared to forget he was running to Kay. He grabbed the chair next to her and started pushing it across the floor.

William lifted Pete and held him against his chest while he stopped crying. It only took a minute. Then he held the baby farther away to smile at him. Pete only stared back. He was going to need more encouragement to smile. William didn't have it in him at the moment. Pete was going to start crawling soon, and William was looking forward to watching him tag after his brother. He couldn't watch if it happened in a different state.

Kay was still looking at her phone on the table. Her eyes darted guiltily back and forth between it and William as though she just couldn't stop. When she noticed him looking at her, she closed her eyes altogether. She turned her back to the table before she opened them. Her mouth worked while she tried to figure out what to say.

Then he realized that it wasn't resignation that made her appear calm. She was holding on by the barest thread, holding herself together so she didn't have to put herself back together. "I'm sorry," William repeated. And meant it even more. Yelling at her had been a dumb move.

"When he called… when he told me they gave the job to someone else, I was so upset… I was so afraid of moving that… I tried to call Beth." She bit hard on her lower lip, trying to keep it from trembling.

"Oh, man." William stepped closer. He wanted to hug her, but she folded her arms, possibly to ward off that exact impulse.

"Of course I remembered I couldn't. I'd barely picked up the phone when I remembered. But still… How could I forget for even a second that she's…" She took a deep breath and rubbed her hands over her eyes, though they looked dry. "Now I can't stop thinking about the fact that her number is still in my phone. Someone else has to have it by now and it feels awful to imagine someone else calling and making her name appear on my screen and I know how incredibly unlikely that is but I still keep thinking it and at the same time, I can't bring myself to delete that contact. I cannot delete my sister."

"I still have my parents' old number. It's not the same thing at all, but that's kind of my point." William's parents had moved to Cleveland a few years earlier, and they gave up a landline in the process. "I just don't want to delete the number because it's the one I had when I was a kid. That's a much stupider reason than the one you have. I say you keep Beth's number, with her name on it, for as long as you want."

Her mouth relaxed a little, which was as close to a smile as anyone could manage at the moment. "Thanks," she said. "I know it's a dumb thing to worry about."

"No, no." William tried to bring back his exact words. Had he accidentally implied that she was dumb? "I said *I* was being dumb."

Then she actually smiled, only briefly. "I know. I mean, I know I'm making a bigger deal of it than it really is because it's easier than worrying about what really is a big deal. I haven't even called my dad yet."

If she hadn't told her dad she was coming, there still had to be a way to stop her. William had been so sure she'd find a job he hadn't spent enough time thinking of other options. He could offer her money, but she'd been so adamant about not asking her dad that he was afraid that would insult her somehow. He thought about following her to Seattle. He couldn't stay with her dad though. He'd have to find a new job himself and sell his house and... It would take weeks and maybe months to arrange everything. And she didn't want to go. How helpful would it really be to follow her where she didn't want to go?

Annie's suggestion came to mind. There wasn't time for that.

He wouldn't take Kay to the courthouse under any circumstances. If he ever talked her into marrying him, they would exchange vows in a church in a proper ceremony. The fact that she'd almost certainly refuse had something to do with holding back the question as well. That really only left one option.

~~~~

This was it. Maybe. William was going to rescue her again. He'd been there for her so many times these last few months. She hoped he was about to save her from a move that scared her, scared her right down to her bones. She didn't want to live with her dad and Sherry in a place she'd never been. Just getting there sounded terrifying. She'd never driven a U-Haul, never driven for days at a time, never traveled with babies, never checked into a hotel by herself.

Katherine Donovan was not the sort of person to seek adventure. She liked repetition and would choose familiar over new in almost every case. She was completely confident that – despite the fear – she could do everything necessary to get to Seattle. But she also knew there would be no sense of accomplishment at the end of the journey, only exhaustion followed by more new experiences and an adjustment period of who knew how long.

Her hopes rose as William was thinking. He'd talked so much about a loan from her dad that she thought he might be working up to offer her one himself. She'd take his money. She'd hate herself for being quantifiably in debt to him, but she'd take it anyway. Maybe he was going to offer now. Or maybe he was going to propose something better.

"Kay, how would you feel about... would you even consider... instead of moving in with your dad, would you consider moving in with me?"

"With you?"

"Only temporarily." He spoke much faster now that he'd gotten out the main idea. "You only plan to live with your dad until you find a job and save enough to get a place of your own. You could do that here if you lived... if you stayed with me. I only have the one extra bedroom so you'd have to share with the boys, but the living space is bigger so you might actually be less cramped than you are here. Oh! And we have benefits for domestic partners so I could get you and the boys on my insurance so that'd be one less thing you'd need to worry about."

"Wouldn't that be kind of dishonest since we're not, uh...?" Kay's face warmed. Why was she blushing out of nowhere? Maybe it was relief.

William shook his head. "I'd only be saying that we live together, and if you actually lived with me there'd be nothing dishonest about it."

Could she really move in with William? It sounded like the answer to her prayers and yet some vague sense of disappointment held her back.

"Don't worry about... I mean, it really wouldn't cost me much. The mortgage payment doesn't go up because a few more people live there, and you know I get takeout all the time. If you were willing to cook for me regularly you might even be saving me money."

That was likely an exaggeration. But it would cost him less than loaning her rent money.

"My house is one story so you wouldn't have to lug the babies up and down the steps anymore. You wouldn't have to find a new church or pediatrician and Annie could still be your babysitter for interviews." William nodded encouragingly at her, encouraging her to agree. He'd apparently run out of arguments and was now ready for an answer.

Kay found herself able to define the disappointment. All of his reasons were about her, about helping her. She liked that William was faithful to a fault. It was amazing to have someone in her life who always put her first. Just this once, she wanted it to be about him. She wanted him to say he would miss her if she left.

"Also…" William thought of something else. "If you move locally, I can help you pack *and* unpack and Chris'll probably let us borrow his truck again so you won't have to deal with a rental. This would be so much easier on you. You have to stay with me."

"Are you sure?" she asked. She was giving him a chance to say it was what he wanted, too.

"Of course. It'll be no trouble." He smiled at Pete in his arms. "And I'm not ready to say goodbye to the little ones."

At least he wanted the babies to stay. That would have to be good enough because she was pretty sure she wasn't physically able to turn down the offer. "Okay," she said.

"Okay? Okay as in yes? Do you want to think about it?"

"I think I like your idea a lot better than moving to Seattle. Unless *you* need to think about it?" She should give him a chance to be sure it wasn't a hasty idea, but her hopes were climbing so fast she might start crying if he changed his mind.

"I wouldn't offer if I wasn't sure."

"We'll have to redo all the plans we made this weekend."

"Piece of cake," he said. William looked so relieved that she could tell he did want her to stay. Maybe just not enough to say it. He was making goofy faces at Pete when he looked up and caught her smiling at him.

Kay was relieved, too. More than she could say. There was something beyond relief, something that let her meet his eyes longer than she could with most people. She studied the bright blue as she thought of how grateful she was and how she loved him. That was definitely a thought she needed to keep to herself. He might misunderstand. There were a lot of kinds of love. She mumbled, "Thank you," then looked away to see what Will was up to.

"Uh... speaking of cake," William said, "you didn't happen to make dessert tonight, did you?"

"Sorry. No." Kay kind of wished she had. She felt like celebrating. She deflated that emotion, at least for a while. She had to let her dad know not to expect her. He knew she'd rather not move, but it would still be better not to sound too excited about not coming to stay with him. "I better call my dad."

William nodded. He put Pete back on his blanket for some more tummy time and sat next to him. Will was crawling across the floor pushing a truck. He veered his path to head towards William.

Kay's dad answered on the first ring. "Kay! What's the verdict?"

"Hi, Dad. Um... well, I didn't get the job *but...* I'm sorry I didn't call you as soon as I found out. I've been working on another option."

"You're not bringing the boys to stay with us." His voice was very matter-of-fact. She couldn't tell if he was disappointed or relieved. She figured he had mixed emotions about the arrangement. He'd love to have her and the grandkids closer, but the same house might be too close.

"I'm going to stay in Ohio. Uh... William said I could stay with him until I find a job."

"You're moving in with your boyfriend?" Now there was clear disappointment.

"No, Dad. He's not my boyfriend." She turned her back on William when she said it. She had the weird feeling that she didn't

95

want to face him while she was lying. It was weird because she said the absolute truth. "He has two bedrooms, and I'll be sharing with Will and Pete."

"Sounds crowded."

"No more than we are here. And it'll only be temporary."

He sort of grunted into the phone before he asked if she needed anything. He told her briefly about a business trip he'd just taken, then asked if she was sure she didn't want to come to Seattle. He assured her his offer would not expire. She politely refused and returned the sentiment when he told her Sherry said hello. Then she hung up and wanted to throw her arms into the air. Staying in Ohio was now official. Instead of silly celebrating, she began to work on dinner. She owed William big and could at least start with hamburgers.

9

"Happy Thanksgiving!" Annie flung open her front door with the greeting. William was holding Pete's car seat. Will wanted to walk on his own so Kay was at the bottom of the porch steps watching him try to step up each step before he put his hands down to help himself. Annie disappeared for a moment to let William inside, then returned to the doorway to grin at Will. "You made it! Good job."

He ran past her into the house.

"Hi, Annie," Kay said. "Happy Thanksgiving."

"Hi. I guess congratulations are in order. William texted that you're staying in town so that must mean you got a job."

"No, um... no, I didn't."

"Oh, I'm sorry. You—" She looked like she was scratching her head though she wasn't literally scratching her head. "Come inside and get warm. Then we'll talk."

Kay rushed in so Annie could shut out the cold wind whipping up the day. There were flurries in the forecast. Kay shivered as she adjusted to the warm house. Annie hadn't said they were going to talk in any kind of ominous way, yet Kay felt something ominous.

William had said on the way over that he'd told everyone she was staying. He had evidently skipped all the details. Why? Was he so casual about it that it didn't matter when his family found out?

Or was he intentionally waiting until Kay was there to make them temper their disapproval.

While it wasn't a lot of people's reality, Kay had been raised to believe you didn't move in with someone of the opposite sex unless you were married. She got the impression William's family expected the same of him. She hoped they could see that this wasn't that. She wasn't moving in with William because of their relationship but because the guy had a hero complex, and she was taking full advantage of him. Maybe that's what she hoped their families didn't see.

Ariana and Bailey crawled past her towards William. "Will you be our owner?" Bailey asked.

William looked at his nieces. "Uh… what?"

"We're playing dogs," Ariana said.

Bailey sat back on her heels to more easily look up at him. "Yeah. We need someone to be our owner."

"Okay. Sit!"

Ariana laughed.

"No," Bailey said. "First you have to come to the pet store to buy us."

"All right." William set Pete's car seat down and followed the crawling girls through the kitchen. "Why is it that every time you girls have me play a game with no rules everything I do is against the rules?"

Kay watched him go, aware that Annie was watching her. She squatted and busied herself getting Pete out of the carrier.

"Can I hold him?" Annie asked.

"Sure." Kay stood and handed him over. Pete was apparently feeling the holiday spirit because he distracted Annie for a while with lots of toothless smiles and tiny squeals.

Jake was in the kitchen. Kay could see his back through the

doorway. Taylor was standing on a stool nearby watching him. There was flour dusted all over the fronts of the lower cabinets. Kay wondered which of them was responsible for the mess.

"Is Jake making the Thanksgiving feast?" Kay asked.

"He, um…" Annie glanced at the kitchen and her face ran through a series of expressions from amusement to annoyance to possibly respect. "He did help," she said. "But now he's… he lost a bet at work and has to make a pie."

Despite the nerves over what she was sure Annie would ask soon, a laugh jumped out of Kay's mouth. "What bet?"

"Oh…" Annie sighed. "It sounded complicated. I guess he and his coworkers were listening to the radio at work and the morning show was asking people to call in to say how long it'd been since they made a pie, like totally from scratch. That got the people at work talking about it, how some of them didn't remember ever doing it. Then later they were going to catch up on some filing before the long weekend and… I guess there was some trash-talking about who had the biggest backlog and they decided to help each other and whoever needed the most help had to make a pie to bring in on Monday. Jake lost. He's making a practice pie today."

"What kind is it?"

"Apple. Because someone said that was the most difficult."

"Wow," Kay said. "Tough crowd."

Annie smiled. "Yeah, I got a text from Jake yesterday that just said he was going to be late because he had to stop at the store for ingredients. He's trying to have it ready to go in the oven when the turkey comes out so it'll still be warm when we eat it. I made a pumpkin one, too."

"I like pumpkin and apple. You guys are setting us up for a hard choice."

"It's Thanksgiving," Annie said with a wink. "Calories don't exist on Thanksgiving. We can eat both."

Ariana had crawled back into the room while her mom was talking. "Do I get both pies, too?"

"Yes, but there are a lot of us. We'll all have small pieces."

Ariana grinned. It kind of looked as though she stopped listening after the first word.

Bailey and William came in next, both also on their hands and knees.

"I thought you were the owner," Kay said.

William gave Bailey a mock scathing glance. "I've been informed that I'm no good at pretending to be a person."

Annie laughed so hard she put her hand over her face.

"We're wild dogs now," Bailey said, "so we don't need an owner. Come on, Woof Woof." She crawled towards the stairs, clearly expecting William, or Woof Woof, to follow her.

The three dogs began to climb up the stairs. William closed a baby gate behind him, which Will had been ignoring until it was open.

Kay came over to pick him up as William gave her an apologetic look. She waved him up the stairs. "Don't worry. I'll find something for Will to do down here."

Kay sat on the floor with Will and pulled a crinkly book from her diaper bag. The stairs he wasn't allowed to climb were soon forgotten.

"I try not to compliment William when he's in the room, but he's really good with kids." Annie was looking towards the stairs, possibly to make sure her brother was out of earshot. She turned back to Kay as her expression got a bit more serious. "I have to ask," she said. She paused before she asked, but Kay guessed what was coming. "I don't want to sound nosy, but you've been saying for weeks that you had to live with your dad after Thanksgiving if you didn't have a job. Now it sounds like something has changed."

That still wasn't a question exactly. "I didn't get the job," Kay said. She took a breath. She would explain as matter-of-factly as possible. That would sound practical and maybe less like she was embarrassed by it. "I was about to call my dad when William said... he offered to let me stay with him instead."

"I see." Annie smiled, almost smugly. She seemed surprisingly *un*surprised.

Had she suspected that Kay was the sort of person who would take advantage of her generous brother? Kay wanted to say that she wasn't normally that kind of person. She felt as though everything that had happened in the past few months had been out of her control, even her own decisions. But using grief as an excuse wasn't right. She felt a need to defend herself and a rising panic that there was no defense. "It's just temporary," she said. "I'm still looking for a job. I mean, it seemed pointless to try to contact anyone during the holiday so we're going to spend the weekend moving my stuff. Monday I'll be looking again. It's just temporary."

"You know I didn't want you to have to leave, Kay."

"It's just temporary," Kay said again. Annie sounded sympathetic and that only made her feel self-conscious about being defensive. "I didn't ask him. He offered."

"I'm sure he did. I—"

"Honey, can you grab Taylor while I have the oven open?"

Annie jumped up and set Pete on the carpet at Jake's request. She stopped at the doorway and turned back. "Please don't think I'm giving you a hard time about this. I might have to give William a hard time, but that's only—"

Something started beeping in the kitchen. Annie shook off whatever else she was going to say to help with the cooking.

Pete made a fussing sound and kicked his legs harder. Kay

moved to lean over him. "Hey, sweetie." She rested a hand on his tummy and spoke softly. "Staying with William seemed like a perfect solution until I started worrying about what other people would think. Why is it every time I start to think we'll be okay, the feeling doesn't last long?"

The baby had no answer of course, but he calmed as he gazed up at her. Will, on the other hand, saw his opportunity to make a break for the kitchen. "I don't think they need your help," Kay said as she swooped an arm around his waist. She pulled him back and very gently tossed him to the ground in a play tackle. He giggled and squirmed to get up. As soon as he was on his feet, he headed towards the kitchen with a glance over his shoulder that said he was more interested in being stopped again than reaching the other room.

Kay grabbed him. He was laughing before she even had him on the ground. She tried not to think of anything outside the moment as both her boys smiled at her. The moment got crowded as three "dogs" returned to the room and Annie soon gathered them all around a fuller than usual table.

Jake asked God to bless the food before he began to carve the turkey. Kay had spent her last few Thanksgivings with Rob and Beth. Rob sliced off enough turkey for everyone in the kitchen where they filled their plates before heading to the dining room. Her heart ached at the memory, but her eyes stayed dry. The familiar faces around her were what kept the tears back. She knew if she was at home spending Thanksgiving alone, she'd be sobbing. That gave her an easy answer when Jake went around the table asking each person what he or she was grateful for that year.

Kay said, "I'm extremely grateful for the invitation to spend Thanksgiving with this family."

William was next to her with Will in a high chair on his other side. "I'm grateful that I didn't have to make any of this wonderful food."

"We're all grateful for that," Annie said.

He simply nodded in agreement with the jab. "And I'm pretty sure Will is grateful specifically for the mashed potatoes." William offered another spoonful to the toddler, who opened his mouth eagerly.

Kay smiled at the other things people said, most of them related to what they were eating. Her smile faltered when she realized they were going around the table a second time. It would be her turn again. She quickly said, "God."

That earned her a lot of nods, so many that she was copied all the way around the table and her next turn came in only a few seconds. "Um..." Kay was grateful for many things. She knew that. It was just really hard to think of them with a roomful of people looking at her. "I, uh... I'm glad I get to stay in Ohio."

"I'm thankful to have a job I don't hate, parents who visit just often enough, and a life that in general isn't missing a whole lot," William said.

He answered before anyone reacted to Kay's statement, not that she expected a big reaction. But she worried he spoke quickly because he was trying to prevent disapproval or other opinions. Then Kay was kicking herself because her gratitude sounded selfish. Freak-outs were a lot like snowballs. If something stuck, it was easy to keep gathering up more worries. She'd never think of anything clever to say.

William tapped the back of her hand at the same time she realized her turn had come already. He didn't squeeze or try to grab it, he simply reached under the table and tapped the back of it with his fingers as he said, "Now I'm grateful that we're done listing our gratitude for today."

The comment earned him a big laugh from his nieces. Jake and Annie let him put an end to it. Kay was still collecting worries and feared he stopped her because she might say something to embarrass him. Or something *else*. What if no one else was all that glad she was staying local? What if she hadn't really been invited for dinner at all? What if William tricked his sister into being host the same way he tricked Kay into accepting? She felt flushed. All those pleasant feelings of sharing Thanksgiving slipped away as she began to wish she could be alone for a while.

Pete made a noise that no one wanted to hear during a meal.

"He pooped!" Ariana said. She was giggling pretty hard.

Bailey gave her sister a disapproving look. She was way too old to find such things amusing.

"Excuse me," Kay said as she pushed back her chair.

William also moved away from the table. "I can change him if you want."

"I got him." Kay didn't look at William as she fled the room, didn't even thank him for the offer to help. She was failing the holiday miserably.

The diaper bag was in the living room. She picked it up and carried it and Pete into a bathroom where she knelt on the floor for a few disgusting minutes of peace. She could hear voices from the kitchen, though not loud enough to understand anything that was said. There were a few quick laughs before she got Pete cleaned up. It sounded as though the others carried on without her. The thought soothed her. If her leaving was barely noticeable, then coming back should be just as unremarkable. She washed her hands and lifted Pete from the floor.

Bailey's voice dominated the conversation as Kay returned to the table. She was explaining a game that she'd been playing recently at recess. Each of her parents gave Kay only a brief glance as she took her seat. But William seemed to stop paying attention to Bailey altogether. He leaned close to Kay and whispered, "You didn't miss much."

His nearness sent an unexpected shiver through her, a shiver of attraction. She smiled to acknowledge his words but had no idea what to do with that other part. A comment on his niece's long-winded story certainly didn't count as flirting. She was puzzled that a little closeness could provoke a reaction. They were always close, passing babies back and forth, sharing meals and almost any time they were both in her tiny apartment. She could not afford to start thinking about William romantically. Literally. She could not afford it. He'd never be comfortable sharing his house if he thought she was feeling mushy towards him, and it might be months before she could pay rent elsewhere.

Kay took a bite of green beans. She hadn't liked them as a kid and even now they were pretty low on her list of edible vegetables. The rubbery texture was a good cure for shivers.

The three girls ran off to play when they'd eaten their fill. The apple pie had just come out of the oven so it was too hot to eat. The adults sat with the babies chatting over empty plates while the pie cooled.

"What are the odds this pie will be worth all the hype?" William asked.

"Oh, it'll be awesome." Jake spoke with confidence, but he smiled in a way that said he boasted in jest.

"As long as it's not a disaster," Annie said. "My kitchen is going to be taken over by practice pies all weekend if this attempt isn't good."

"Now I don't know what to hope for." William sat back and put on a look of concentration. "I love a good apple pie, but a good pie disaster... that might be fun to bring up at, like, every

Thanksgiving from now on." He shared a laugh with the women while Jake pretended to glare through a laugh of his own.

"Seriously, guys," Jake said. "I don't expect my first attempt to be the best dessert anyone's ever eaten, but I followed a pretty highly rated recipe. It should be good."

"We've probably teased Jake about the pie enough, at least until we've tasted it," Annie said, preparing to change the subject. "So William?"

"Yes?" He was wiping off Will's hands to pull him from the high chair to his lap, but he sent his sister an expectant glance.

"I hear you're cleaning out your extra bedroom."

Kay had been relaxed during the pie discussion. She tensed again. This was going to be about her.

"Not much to clear out really," William said nonchalantly. "A few boxes and odds and ends. I put most of it in the garage since I... Oh, wait." He turned to Kay. "I need to give you a place to park."

She shook her head. "I can park on the driveway or the street."

"No, I'll clear the garage." He pushed his plate and utensils out of the toddler's reach. "If your car sits out, you'll have to scrape frost off it all the time."

"I do that now," Kay said.

"That's because you don't have an option."

"I can't expect you to move all the stuff again."

"Yes, you can." He gave a quick sigh. "It's my fault for not thinking it through sooner."

"I'll park on the street."

"No. I'll feel bad if you and the babies are dealing with frost because of a few stupid boxes, and I know you won't let me give up my spot so the only solution is to put the boxes somewhere else."

"Right."

Kay and William both looked at Annie because she packed a ton of sarcasm into that one word.

"That's the only solution because it's the *only* problem," she said. Annie had said she might give William a hard time about their decision, but Kay hadn't expected to be in the room when it happened. The tension made her realize how calmly she'd been talking to William even when their words had bordered on an argument. It was a strange thought, and she didn't have much time for it. Pete was falling asleep in her arms. Maybe she could look for a place to put him down if she stayed the topic of conversation for long. Then again, maybe she'd rather *know* what Annie thought rather than imagine it.

"What other problem might you be referring to?" William asked.

"I think you know, and I think it stems from the fact that my brother doesn't want to take my advice."

William tipped his head in a very good impression of a confused person. "Why are we talking about Michael all of a sudden?"

"Not that brother," Annie said quickly, then pinched her lips together to keep from smiling.

William did smile. It helped Kay a little, helped her remember that William was on her side. Even if Annie was preparing some disapproving remarks, William was on her side.

"There's only a problem if you make one," he said.

"Why would you think I'd make a problem?"

"Because you have a lot of dumb ideas."

"You followed at least one of my ideas."

"That's how I know it was dumb."

Annie glanced at Kay. "Maybe not everyone would think it was dumb."

"Annie." There was a sudden note of warning in William's voice.

Annie raised her eyebrows playfully in response. "You *could* ask," she said.

"I think Will is getting sleepy." William stood from the table holding the toddler, who did seem to be wilting. "Can I put him in Taylor's crib?"

"Yeah. I don't think she's going to nap today." Annie switched gears so fast it was as though they'd been talking about kids and naps all along.

"I'll walk him around for a minute before I put him down," William said, mostly to Kay, "so you can start dessert without me if I'm not back."

"Hey, that's a good idea." Jake excused himself from the table with a stack of used plates.

Annie leaned forward when only the two women were left at the table. "Don't worry," she said. "I really don't have a problem. I just like to watch William squirm."

Kay nodded. She really had no idea what the siblings had been going on about, but she felt genuinely reassured by Annie's words, reassured that whatever it was didn't have anything to do with her taking advantage of William after all. She became aware of the weight of Pete on her arm and the fact that he was cutting off the circulation in her hand. "I think I'd like to try to put Pete down somewhere, too."

"Good idea." Annie stood up faster since she was not holding a baby. "I'll finish clearing so we can have dessert when you get back."

Jake was at the other end of the room standing over his pie. He was either preparing to cut it or studying it for signs of weakness. He looked up as Kay walked past. "Pumpkin, apple or both?" he asked.

"Both," she said. Then stepped into the quiet room. That had seemed like a good place to leave the baby since she'd see the girls going through the kitchen and know if they might be about to disturb him. But two of the girls were already in there. Bailey was reading Cinderella to Ariana. They looked sweet squashed into a beanbag together.

Before Kay even had time to consider if it might be better to put Pete elsewhere, Bailey closed the book and said, "Daddy's getting dessert!"

Ariana was in the kitchen in two seconds. Bailey worked to cram her book onto a very full bookshelf before she followed.

"Guess it'll be nice and quiet for you at least for a while," Kay whispered. She squatted and placed him on the carpet in the corner of the room. She pulled the rag off her shoulder and draped it over his legs. She wasn't worried about him being cold in his blanket sleeper. The placement was only so she'd know where to find the rag when she came back to pick him up.

She'd been holding her breath as she put him down because he'd be mad if he woke up. The little guy barely stirred as she pulled her hands out from under him. She slowly exhaled and took a moment to watch his tiny sleeping face. Someday he would be old enough to read those books, too. She knew that was true, but somehow the thought puzzled her all the same. She couldn't imagine him beyond the baby he was right then.

Kay was the last one, besides William, to return to the table for pie. She quickly took a bite of the apple one first in case anyone asked her opinion. If the question did come up, she would not have to lie or even try diplomacy. The pie was heavy on the cinnamon and cloves she'd smelled while it was baking. The spices made friends with her taste buds.

No one asked Kay about the pie though. Instead, Bailey looked at her and said, "Are you going to marry Uncle William?"

Kay shook her head no. It was an innocent, matter-of-fact question and she gave an innocent, matter-of-fact answer.

That wasn't good enough for Bailey. "Why not?" she asked.

"I... well, we're friends." Kay winced a little at what was probably not a very good answer. She couldn't think of a better one.

"Mommy says you should be friends with someone before you get married." Bailey's eyes turned the statement into a question, or perhaps a dare.

"Yeah," Kay said slowly. Maybe she could follow Bailey into general territory. "It's definitely a good idea to marry someone you get along well with. A friend."

"Okay. So you're gonna marry William later?"

"Um... I don't know."

"You like him, don't you?" Bailey looked confused.

"I do." She liked William a lot. There was no reason to be coy about it. "It's just that... well... I guess I've never really thought about marrying him."

"Oh. You should."

"I guess I can think about it." Kay thought agreeing would end the interrogation. She glanced at Jake and Annie to see if either of them was going to tell their daughter to be less nosy. Jake was shoveling pie into his mouth. Annie was watching as though she was just as interested in Kay's answers as Bailey. No help appeared to be coming.

Bailey was shaking her head. "No, I don't mean think about it. I mean you should marry him. I've never been to a wedding."

Where was William when she needed him? Kay knew he would just throw in a joke or casually change the subject. She couldn't figure out how to do either. Maybe she could turn the spotlight on him. "Well, he'd have to agree. I don't know if William would even want to marry me."

"Ask him," Bailey said.

"It's, uh… it's tradition for the guy to ask so I can't." There. She couldn't ask him. End of uncomfortable, personal discussion.

The answer did seem to satisfy Bailey. She stabbed a bite of pie.

The whole table was quiet as William walked into the room. "That took longer than it should have," he said. "Looks good in here." He eyed the dessert set at his place. His hand grabbed the back of his chair to pull it out.

"Ask Kay to marry you," Bailey said.

William's hand froze on the chair as his eyes darted around the table trying to determine if her command was as out of the blue as it seemed or if he'd missed something.

A tiny snort drew Kay's attention. Annie was trembling violently against a laugh that wanted out. Everyone was looking at her, all of them a little confused. All except William, who was looking at her so hard his eyes might have been trying to bore holes in her. He said, "Shut. Up."

That did her in. Annie burst with laughter as she jumped from the table. She fled into another room to get herself under control.

William sighed as he took his seat.

Bailey and Ariana looked at their dad to see what was so funny. Kay turned that way as well. Jake shrugged at them.

"Pie's good," William said. Then he turned casually to Bailey. "Where'd you get the idea I should ask Kay to marry me?"

"I like weddings," she said.

He nodded. "What do you like about weddings?"

"The cake. And everyone wears pretty clothes."

"Even the guys?"

She wrinkled her nose. "Not the guys. I like dresses."

113

William talked to her about where she'd seen these pictures of weddings and soon they were chatting about other books. Annie returned at some point, completely calm again.

Kay marveled at how William had so easily gotten away from anything personal. How had he done that? And why was she disappointed that he had?

10

$\mathcal{K}$ay opened her eyes and shook off a bit of disorientation. It took her only a few seconds to remember where she was. William's house. The windows in this bedroom had light coming at her from a different direction than at her apartment. It was only a hint of light, only what the streetlight on the corner sent her way.

Pete was crying.

She rolled out of bed and lifted him out of his crib. She held him close, making soft shushing noises. She squinted at the clock by her bed. It was barely 2 AM. Pete had slept through the night more often than not the last few weeks, but she'd expected that the unfamiliar house might disturb him.

Kay used to come to William's house fairly regularly. They'd mostly alternated where they got together before Beth died. She hadn't been to his house since the babies came to live with her until the Friday after Thanksgiving – two days ago – when they'd brought the first load of her belongings. They'd made a few trips with her car on Friday. Then Chris brought his truck again on Saturday to move all the large items.

She'd been oddly shocked to realize she'd be staying the night on Saturday. Her brain had somehow calculated that they'd spend the whole weekend moving her stuff, then she and the boys would move in on Monday. She'd been putting together the second crib when reality clicked into place. It made no sense to sleep at her apartment once their beds had been moved.

Even when she'd been there regularly though, she'd never been in either bedroom. Kay paced with Pete, trying to calm him when she didn't feel completely calm herself in the foreign room. The walls were white. Her old bedroom was light blue. This room had a different smell, too. It was a better smell if she was honest. Her apartment had been in an old house, and it had a slightly musty smell.

Kay nuzzled closer to Pete for his familiar sweet baby scent. He wasn't crying anymore. He was sort of grunting and fussing as he mashed his face against her shoulder. She hoped he was trying to get comfortable to go back to sleep. Morning was still several hours away. They both needed to get back to sleep.

Kay wondered if William had heard the crying. There was a short hallway outside her bedroom with a bathroom and laundry room on either side of it. The hallway led to the kitchen, which made an el with the living room. William's bedroom was on the other side of that. It might be a good enough buffer zone, but it really depended entirely on how easily William woke. Little Will was in the next crib and hadn't given any sign he was aware of the movement around him.

"Thank you, God," Kay whispered. "Thank you for making Will a good sleeper." She paused, thinking that was a weird reason to thank God. She'd never thought of sleeping as something people could be good at. "I'm just glad that... I love these babies, but I don't know if I have the patience to handle both in the middle of the night." She wasn't entirely sure it was patience that got her up anyway. It was more like conditioning. Her head felt heavy and foggy as though only waiting for the pillow to be asleep again.

Pete was showing signs that Kay could put him down. She placed him in the crib and watched the precious baby as she stood straight. He threw one arm and leg over the other but didn't fully turn over. She smiled at the idea that he was trying to be like his brother.

Morning arrived with Kay unable to remember going back to bed. She was in her bed though. A snippet of a dream was fading to prove she'd even been asleep. There was a bench and a park that didn't look like a place she'd ever been. She let go of the image to wake herself up. She sat up and looked at her boys. They were both awake. Will was watching her. He stood up and smiled when he saw that she was getting up. Pete was crying. It wasn't a miserable cry but the kind that wanted attention.

He began to settle as he saw Kay approach. "Morning, guys. You know it's still dark, right?" She pulled Will out first so he could walk next to her as she carried Pete. She'd thought – or hoped rather – that the boys were early risers in the summer because the sun woke them. But they'd stayed consistent even into late November when there was no sunlight at 6:30.

Will charged from the bedroom as she opened the door. Kay hurried after him, hoping that cereal would keep him quiet enough not to wake William. But William was already sitting at the kitchen table with a book and a cup of coffee. He looked up, gave something like half a nod, then lowered his eyes to his book again.

The good morning Kay had been about to utter stopped halfway up her throat. The normal William had been replaced by a guy who didn't look receptive to her presence, let alone her greeting.

Kay's fingers began to tremble as she took a bowl out of a cupboard to feed Will. She knew where things were kept because she'd eaten there before. But in the past, she'd opened cupboards feeling as though she was helping William. Now she felt as though she was helping herself to his things. Why the surly demeanor? Did he regret offering his place already?

Will hollered and pointed. Kay tried to ignore William – a hopeless endeavor – to focus on Will. Letting the little guy get upset would not help anyone's mood. The toddler yelled, "Want it," and pointed again at the line of cereal boxes.

Kay held up a box.

He shook his head and continued to point.

She held up another box.

Will smiled and ran to his high chair. The toddler was adorable tugging on the front as he tried to climb into it. He was near William though, who didn't seem amused. Kay was overwhelmed by a confusing desire to make a good impression on the guy she'd known for years. She hurried over to help Will into the chair. Then she hurried to put a bowl in front of him and fill it with cereal. She pulled a bottle out of the fridge for Pete and a sippy cup of milk for Will.

He looked up at her with a curious expression when she set the cup on his tray. The little guy had evidently noticed that she wasn't narrating her every move as she usually did. It had never seemed like a weird habit. In fact, it made sense to talk in front of the babies to help them learn how. But William's quiet trance made her second guess everything, especially what he might or might not think was weird.

Kay sat on the other side of the table and got Pete started on his bottle. He put his little hands on either side of the bottle as though he wanted to hold it himself. She smiled slightly and her mouth froze in that position as she glanced up. William had closed his book. He had frown lines on his forehead as he peered into the bottom of his mug. The sight should have continued Kay's feeling of intimidation, but Will was right next to him trying to copy the expression.

Kay tried to see William as her little boy saw him. The man

had bare toes peeking out of too long pajama bottoms. His t-shirt was wrinkled and his hair messy. A ring of coffee on the table said he'd filled his cup sloppily. Then she looked at his eyes. They weren't squinted in anger but rather still trying to open fully.

Quite suddenly, William stopped looking like a belligerent landlord and morphed into a friend who was just grumpy because it was morning. He turned his head slowly to face the toddler who was imitating him. The pair of them were so charming with their matching frowns that Kay had to look away to keep from laughing out loud. She grinned at Pete, who stopped sucking long enough to smile back.

"I need a shower," William said, his voice gravelly.

He put his mug in the sink. His hand passed gently over the top of Will's head as he moved out of the room. When he'd closed his bedroom door behind himself, Kay resumed a normal breakfast routine. She gave Will a play-by-play as she gathered a bowl of cereal for herself and asked if he was ready for more. She talked to Pete, too. She assured him that she'd never drop him no matter how many times she needed to shift him around.

The babies had been getting baths after breakfast on Sundays. The sides on the tub were slightly higher. It was a difference she wouldn't notice by sight. But the slippery Will was a bit harder to reach as she knelt near him. She had to pull clothes for the boys from boxes she'd yet to unpack. And when she picked out a dress for herself, Kay was aware that the door opened on a hinge rather than sliding on a track like the one at her apartment. The bar was higher. Her shoes fit inside the closet. Both her laundry baskets were full of stuff she didn't know where to store, which meant there was a growing pile of dirty clothes in the corner of the room.

Kay's life looked drastically different than it had three months ago. And it was still a mess. Her mind was focusing on all the upheaval of the last three days. Everything was different. Again. She tried not to think that her living arrangement was intended as temporary. Temporary meant more change was coming.

The only change Will was concerned about was when the bedroom door was going to be opened for him. He grabbed for the handle then looked back to make sure Kay saw what he wanted.

"One minute, honey," she said. A quick glance around the room confirmed that all three of them were dressed. Kay tugged the rubber band off the end of her hair so the braid would begin to come undone. She took Pete from his crib before she let Will out so they could follow close behind. William had tried to get his house ready for babies, but Kay already knew that no place could be considered babyproof until a baby had been let loose to point out what had been missed.

William was sitting on the floor in the living room with a pile of blocks. He had a colorful tower in front of him and was balancing a block on top as Kay rounded the corner. Will ran directly to the tower and sent everything crashing to the ground. William laughed and encouraged the little guy to help him build another one.

William was dressed for church as well. His face was smooth and his hair still damp. He wore a familiar dark green shirt with a black stripe across the chest. Kay was pretty sure he only had three church-worthy shirts that he constantly cycled through on Sundays. She thought he'd worn the green one just the last week.

She smiled. It was a reminder that there were some constants in her life. God was with her through all the turmoil of course, but William was there, too. Their bond had strengthened with his continual presence. She felt safe enough to yell at him and let him see her in the ugliest cry. And that same old green shirt brought a moment of unexpected happiness.

"Twenty minutes?" he said.

Kay looked at the clock before she nodded. They did have a little time before they needed to leave for church. It was likely around the time William had been leaving when he drove to Kay's first to ride with her. Kay tried to tell herself that leaving together was one way her moving in would help William. She didn't believe it. She knew he didn't have to go to church with her at all.

It was a good Sunday in the sense that all four of them stayed in the church until the closing hymn. That was a feat they'd been accomplishing more often. Pete was generally happy being held and sometimes even fell asleep. Will liked to move though. Staying in one place for more than an hour was hard on him and hard for those trying to help him through it. The trick, it seemed, was to have William hold Pete while Kay let Will climb on and off her lap repeatedly.

William said it worked because she was a calming influence. Kay suspected Will was more often quiet with her only because he expected William to be more fun. Regardless, she praised Will on the way out for not disturbing anyone else too much.

Because Kay was driving, William read the bulletin on the way home. "Hey!" he said. "Look at this."

"Uh... I'm driving."

"I didn't mean actually look at it, I meant... they're advertising an open position in the church office. Twenty to twenty-five hours a week. Some pretty basic computer skills. You could do this."

"I couldn't save up enough to move out on a part-time income."

"How much money are you making *now*?" William asked. His tone said the answer was obvious. And it was.

Kay nodded to acknowledge her lack of income. "Okay. So

part-time is better than no-time. I bet they're not offering insurance."

"You don't need it. I got you and the boys covered. And it says apply to Mrs. Adams for more info. I think you'd like working with her."

Mrs. Adams had been at the church forever. Kay could remember her getting all the boys and girls lined up during their First Communion practice. And when she needed service hours in high school, Mrs. Adams had a list of suggestions that worked for shy kids. She had kind words for everyone and would be a great boss. "I like Mrs. Adams, but—"

"You should call her," William said. "This job sounds good for you and a part-time job would mean part-time day care so... less expense." He sort of winced at the end of his sentence. He clearly knew that the job would still not be enough to support three people. Yet he seemed eager for Kay to take it.

She found herself more excited about the prospect of working in the church office than any of the other places she'd applied. People, and Kay knew she was no exception, did have a habit of wanting things that were not in their best interest. She couldn't take a job only because she wanted it. This required real thought.

She couldn't move out without a full-time job that would support all three of them. She'd been failing for a month already though. How much debt would she be racking up with William while she hunted one? Her bank balance was getting scary. They had expenses beyond the roof William was providing. Will was outgrowing his clothes. They'd agreed that Kay would do the grocery shopping. If she didn't have *some* income, she'd have to start asking William for money to buy food.

On the other hand, taking a job she might have to quit in a month or two felt wrong. She needed some guidance.

Then Kay realized that she was thinking about this job as though it had already been offered to her. There was an easy way to let God in on the decision. "I'll call Mrs. Adams tomorrow," she said. "And if the job goes to someone else, I'll know it wasn't meant to be."

"You'll get it," William said. He sounded confident. He sounded as though he fully believed it was meant to be. Maybe that was only because it was his idea.

11

William wasn't sure what had woken him. He didn't hear any clatter or loud bumps. There did appear to be some movement in the kitchen though. He squeezed his eyes shut, thinking that might help them spring open. No such luck. He tried to focus his foggy brain on what day it was. Christmas. It was Christmas morning and even that thought didn't rouse him.

He'd expected Kay to try for some extra sleep with the boys out of the house. Perhaps that was exactly why she couldn't sleep though.

William pushed back his blanket and sat up. A heavy sigh came from somewhere inside him before he could stand up. He pulled open his door to peek out. Kay was sitting at the table with a book and an empty bowl in front of her. Her hand stopped with a glass of water halfway to the table as she spotted him.

"Oh, no," she said. "Did I wake you?" Her voice was apologetic but her expression suggested she was trying not to laugh at him.

William couldn't decipher the mismatch any more than he could process the fact that she'd just asked a question.

"Go back to bed," she instructed. "I'll be really quiet, and I can even reset the timer on the coffee if you want."

He pulled in a breath, trying to find himself the strength for words. "Leave it," he said. He'd already set it back an hour, and it was a bad idea to get too far off the routine. He stepped back and closed the door. As long as he had a few minutes, he might as well get in a shower before the coffee was ready.

The smell of coffee woke William again. He must have gone back to bed instead of into the shower. He sat up again and staggered towards the kitchen. Kay came from somewhere and handed him a hot mug. He grunted something that he hoped sounded like, "Thank you."

He sat at the table and took a few sips before he opened a book. He kind of liked to stare at a page for a minute before he tried to read it. Kay had smiled when she handed him the coffee. He didn't know how she was such a morning person. She seemed almost amused by morning. That was a concept he couldn't grasp, particularly when morning was so heavily upon them.

After coffee and a shower, William began to feel like himself. And he began to feel remiss in not asking Kay how she was feeling. "Well... Merry Christmas," he said.

"Merry Christmas to you," she answered. She was sitting on the couch folding tiny clothes.

"I'm not sure you should be doing chores on Christmas."

"I have to do something," she said. "Otherwise I'll just be sitting here thinking about how empty the house is."

"It was generous of you to let Rob's parents have the boys for Christmas."

She bunched up the shirt she was about to fold and looked sideways at William. "Yes. It was so *generous* to let them babysit."

William ignored her self-deprecating tone. He knew that she knew they didn't think of it as babysitting but as spending time with grandkids they didn't get to see all that often.

Kay sighed and resumed folding the shirt. "I suppose this is better than if they had invited me to bring the boys. I know I can't get to know them without spending more time with them but… I'd hate to make Christmas awkward. Maybe if they lived closer I'd try harder. At least they were careful to say they were only asking about this year and not trying to establish…" She stopped talking and crumpled another shirt. "I can't believe how much I miss them. My rational brain is saying they are safe and happy and I should enjoy the break. But I can't relax. I keep thinking I'm forgetting to take care of someone."

"Maybe it'll help when we get to my sister's. It won't be nearly as quiet there."

"Are you sure I won't be in the way?" She focused more intently on the laundry than before, as though preparing for the fact that any answer was about to make her uncomfortable.

"Yes," William said, trying to pound sincerity into the word and not exasperation. "Annie invited me *and* you before I'd even given a thought to what we'd do for Christmas."

Kay kept her hands working but managed to cast a brief, highly skeptical glance his way.

"Really," he said. "I promise you are welcome." He'd tricked her one time. One time he got her to agree to something without the full story and now she suspected him of manipulating everyone.

"And your parents aren't going to say anything about… They're not upset that I live with you?"

"You lost your job right after getting two extra mouths to feed. I'm pretty sure they'd have helped out any of their friends the same way. You have nothing to worry about."

She nodded but didn't look convinced. Maybe she didn't really suspect him of anything underhanded. Maybe she was only nervous and looking for a way out. This probably wasn't going to be a very merry Christmas for Kay no matter what. She'd been down all week. William thought she was having second thoughts about sending her babies away, but when he asked her she admitted it was Christmas shopping that was depressing her. She'd done her shopping with Beth for as long as she could remember.

William hadn't known how to help or even what to say. He still didn't know what to say. For days he wondered if he should offer himself as an incredibly poor substitute. It was too late now, and he wanted to know how she'd fared. Was asking how she'd managed the shopping on her own just rubbing in the fact that he hadn't helped? Or did it show he at least offered her sympathy? Maybe it didn't matter because he couldn't stop himself from asking.

"How did your Christmas shopping turn out? Were you able to find something for everyone on your list?"

"Yeah, I guess. I mean, I did. I just don't know if they're good presents. And the ones for Sherry and my dad are going to be late. I should have waited until they got here."

Her dad was staying in Seattle for Christmas and coming to visit Kay the first week of January.

"Well, at least if they don't open the presents in front of you, it'll be easier to pretend they like them."

Kay smiled, but she said, "That's not funny."

"I know." He did like to see her smile, even if it was only briefly. "You could blame the lateness on the post office."

"Too late. I already apologized to my dad for mailing them so late."

"Kay Donovan, you are too honest for your own good."

A smile bloomed slowly on her face. It brought a hint of spirit to her eyes. "Too honest?" she said. "When we see your parents, I'll be sure to tell them you think honesty is a bad thing."

He tried to match her mood, to prolong it. "You're going to tattle on me?"

"Maybe I'll wait to see if you do anything to deserve it."

"What could I—"

"Oh, no." The amusement disappeared. "I didn't get your parents anything."

"You barely know my parents. They're not expecting you to get them gifts."

"But I got something for you and Annie and the girls so I had to get something for Jake. Then I got something for Michael so I'll have a present for everyone in your family *except* your parents. That's not right."

"You got Michael something?"

"I know I don't know him well either, but when I found out I'd see him Christmas Day it seemed like a good idea." She shrugged. The shrug asked if it was a good idea.

It was. Michael was twenty-two, but he was still a lot like a kid and kids got presents on Christmas. His parents were both over fifty. They were not kids. "What did you get Michael?" William asked.

"You said he liked cowboy stuff so I got him a big belt buckle with a horse on it. Is that—"

"He'll love it." In fact, he'd probably like it more than what William got him. "And my parents will think it's sweet that you thought of him. That will be enough of a present for them."

"But I should have…" Kay fell against the back of the sofa and knocked over the neat stack of folded baby clothes. She didn't appear to notice. "I was so distracted when I was shopping. It seemed like no matter where I looked I saw something Beth would have liked. Everywhere." Her eyes filled with water and her fingers paused under one eye as though trying to catch tears before they fell.

William put his arm along the back of the couch, an invitation for the hug she might need. She hadn't collapsed against him since the first few weeks after Beth died, but he was prepared to let it happen again.

Kay, however, was not. She backed up and said, "If you hug me, I'm only going to cry for real."

She made it sound as though it would be his fault, and he certainly didn't want to make her cry. But if she needed to cry, he knew she'd rather cry now than later in front of his family. He asked, "Are you sure that's bad?"

She shook her head but did not move any closer. "I think… I think maybe I should be alone today."

"No way. I can't let you do that."

"You can't *let* me?"

William might have regretted his choice of words except that the touch of annoyance made Kay look less defeated. "You know what I mean," he said. "What kind of person would I be if I left you here alone and depressed on Christmas? I can hear my mom lecturing me already."

Kay's lips twitched as she conceded that her absence would put him in an awkward spot. It looked as though she wanted to say something, or explain something.

William knew then that he was an idiot for thinking the sadness was all about Beth. Christmas had already been difficult for Kay because her mom died in December. She'd said once that she and Beth had a tradition for remembering her. William hadn't asked about it at the time because it felt too personal. But now, when he thought that he might be inadvertently standing in the way of that tradition, it felt like his business. Especially when he'd just mentioned his own mom as though he wasn't terribly lucky to still have her around. "How did… what did you and Beth do for your mom on Christmas?"

"It's stupid," she said.

"Now I have to argue with you again because you cannot possibly remember your mom in a way that is stupid."

"You say that like you're happy to have an excuse to argue with me."

"And you say that like you're stalling."

"We take... took..." Kay stopped, took a breath, then started over. "When my mom was little, her parents always bought cereal in bags instead of boxes. She thought that the cereal ended up with a lot more crumbs on the bottom. She said she was always begging her parents to get boxes to protect the cereal and they thought she just imagined the bags had more crumbs. She used to tell me and Beth that we were lucky she wasn't giving us crumby cereal and would shudder when she saw them at the store."

Kay had the faraway look of someone deep in a memory. "I think she exaggerated how much it bothered her just, you know, to be funny. At some point, Beth and I started getting her cereal – in a box – for Christmas. I think it was something we could afford with our meager allowance money. Then around the time I started high school, we realized it was kind of a silly gift. Beth had a job. We pooled our money to get her something nicer, but we kept giving her a box of cereal with whatever else we got. We thought that was funny, and Mom used to laugh. She seemed to enjoy guessing which type she was about to unwrap. Then the year Mom died... Beth had already bought a box of cereal."

Kay paused for a moment. She picked up the clothes she'd knocked over earlier and set them inside the laundry basket. She was stalling again. William waited for her to continue.

"We took the cereal to the cemetery at Christmas," Kay said. "We were going to leave it there with the flowers Dad had. But then we realized... it was snowing... the box would get wet and...so we opened it and sprinkled cereal on the grave. We figured birds would eat it so we wouldn't have to come back to clean up the remains of the box." She lifted her eyes from the baby clothes to William tentatively. "We've been pouring cereal every Christmas since. I told you it was stupid."

"We'll leave early for Annie's to stop at the cemetery on the way. Unless you'd rather go by yourself. In that case, I'll wait for you."

"I'm afraid I'll end up bringing people down if—"

"You're coming with me. I'm happy to give you some space to... I'll even try to keep my family from talking to you too much, but you're not spending Christmas alone."

Kay's eyes looked watery. He was worried he'd been too demanding. She stood rather suddenly and picked up the basket of clothes. "I'll be ready in a few minutes." She flashed a sad smile – it still looked like gratitude – as she walked away. Maybe he could squeeze a little merry into her day by the end of it.

It had snowed a week earlier. Most of it had melted, but gray patches remained along the street towards the cemetery. The sky was thick with clouds so the leftover snow wasn't the only gray. The cemetery was looped with one-lane gravel roads that forced cars to proceed slowly for practical reasons if consideration for mourners wasn't enough. William drove at a snail's pace while the stones crunched and popped beneath his tires. He knew where Kay's mom was buried because it was near Beth and Rob, and he'd been to their funeral.

There was another car parked a short distance ahead on the lane. A young family was gathered around a grave two or three rows from Kay's mom. William wasn't sure from a distance which one was hers, but he knew they were in the right area. Kay was staring out the window.

"Let's wait for them to leave," she said.

He didn't know if she was worried about intruding on the other people's grief or if she didn't want them to see hers. He also didn't know if he was supposed to stay in the car. "All right," he said.

The family had already started moving towards their car, hurrying and hugging themselves against the cold.

Kay opened her door.

"Do you want me to wait or..."

She glanced over her shoulder. "Come with me."

The plea was a welcome one. A command to stay would have been fine as well. William only wanted to feel as though she was being honest and not saying what was arbitrarily appropriate. He could see that she wanted his company.

They walked up to her mother's headstone. William tried to stay a step behind to follow Kay's lead. After a few moments of silence, Kay said, "Um... let's go over... uh..." She moved to the back of the row and stood over the double plot of Elizabeth and Robert Fisher.

Kay shivered.

William zipped his coat.

"Hi, Beth. Merry Christmas." Kay hugged a box of cereal to her chest. "I brought the cereal. I... I think this might be the last time because I don't want to do it without you. What do you think? Is that a good way to end the tradition?" Kay paused. She wasn't waiting for an answer, just thinking about what else to say.

William waited quietly. He pulled his hat a little lower around his ears. Kay was wearing earmuffs. They were light pink and very pretty against her brown hair. Yet he couldn't help thinking they were an odd choice for someone who tried to be invisible most of the time. She was the only person he knew who wore earmuffs.

"I'll think of something better for both of you next year. And you, too, Rob. But for now…" Her breath was visible on the air as she spoke, then a foggy gust appeared as she ran out of words. She began to fumble with the cereal box. Her gloves were preventing her from getting a finger under the cardboard flap.

William pulled his own gloves off. "Let me help you."

She nodded. But instead of passing the box, she tucked it into the crook of her arm to tug at her gloves. "Can you hold my gloves?" She got them off and handed them to William.

Kay's gloves were the same shade of pink as her earmuffs. They were warm when he took them, but the heat dissipated rapidly. He stood there with cold hands holding four gloves while Kay broke open the inner bag.

He watched her sprinkle cereal over her sister's grave. She let some stray onto Rob's side. Then she sort of nodded a confirmation and moved back to her mother's grave. William followed, hands still freezing, still holding four gloves.

"Merry Christmas, Mom." Kay held up the cereal. "I guess you know why I'm here. I, um… I…" She poured a small pile by the headstone. Then she looked at William with a strange expression on her face. "It's not the same without Beth," she said.

"It's not… helping?" Helping was probably the wrong word. He was concerned that she wasn't getting what she expected from her memorial.

She pursed her lips thoughtfully before she said, "It is and it isn't."

Maybe she understood what he meant, but William didn't. He waited to see if she planned to explain.

"I'm glad I did this so I'd know that… with Beth, this felt like… it was a way to share a good memory of Mom. Without Beth, I… I just feel sort of like a crazy person." She glanced at the box she was holding, and a brief laugh escaped. Her hand came up to cover it the same time her eyes filled with tears.

William didn't know if she was trying not to laugh, trying not to cry, or already doing both. Quite positive he couldn't say the right thing when faced with such complex emotions, he stepped closer and put his arms loosely around her. It was more like patting her shoulders than hugging her. Both her arms and a cereal box were between them anyway. He wondered if she kept them there to maintain the distance. Then her head dropped so that her forehead rested on his shoulder.

All other consciousness drifted from his mind. For weeks and weeks Kay had been so close but just out of reach. Now he was holding her, and she was letting him. He didn't hear laughs or sobs from her either, only peace. It was a moment that could go on and on. Except that there was an awful lot of cold seeping into the moment. It stung his fingers and sent chills throughout his body. Kay must be cold, too.

"Are you ready to go?" he asked.

Her head moved. He thought it was a nod but she stayed very still.

Maybe he needed to move first.

William took his arms back as Kay stood straighter.

"Now we face your family," she said. "If you're *sure* they want me to come."

He groaned as he handed her gloves back.

12

Kay continued fretting about not having presents for William's parents all the way to his sister's house. She only mentioned it once, enough for him to know it was on her mind. Then she sat in deep concentration as though a gift would materialize if she thought about it hard enough. He couldn't spend much time convincing her everything would be fine because he was too caught up in his own Christmas dilemma.

The gift he got Kay suddenly felt wrong. Maybe not wrong exactly. He just wasn't sure it was something he wanted her to open in front of his family. But saving it for when they were alone might suggest something that, while true, he wasn't prepared to suggest.

To give himself more time to think about it, William stuffed the tiny package for Kay into his coat pocket while they were unloading the presents from his trunk.

Jake came outside to hold the door open for Kay and William. "Hurry up, hurry up," he said. He was wearing short sleeves and bouncing up and down on his heels to generate heat. He also had a big gold bow stuck to the front of his shirt. William smiled at the jumping bow but did try to get inside as quickly as he could. Jake stepped inside, then pulled the outer door closed. He didn't even glance at the bow as he said, "Taylor put it on me."

"Should we put these under the tree or—"

"More presents!" Ariana yelled across the room.

Bailey ran up and grabbed a present in each hand. "I'll pass them out," she said, "because I can read."

"Hang on." William looked between Bailey and her dad. "Do you want to do more presents right away?" he asked.

Jake shrugged. "You brought 'em. It's up to you."

Three pairs of eyes looked eagerly at William as all his nieces had gathered for the prospect of presents. He tried to ascertain Kay's take on the situation. She shrugged at him, too.

Then a young man stepped out of the kitchen wearing what appeared to be a brand new cowboy hat. Michael took medication that sometimes affected his balance. Anyone who didn't know that might have thought he was practicing his mosey. Then again, he might have been practicing his mosey.

"Merry Christmas, Michael," William said. "It's good to see you."

"Christmas?" Michael said. "I got so many presents I can't get into my room."

"That could be a problem." William smiled, only because he knew it wasn't a problem.

Bailey waved a package with blue snowman paper in front of her uncle to remind him she was waiting for permission to pass them out. "This one's for Michael," she said.

"All right. Let's all—"

"Ohh!" His mother's excitement preceded her into the room. "I knew I heard your voice. Come on." She motioned William forward. "Let's get all those gifts put down so I can get a hug."

Bailey was the first to follow her Gamma Di, with her sisters close on her heels, because Gamma Di now seemed to be in charge of when the presents would be opened. William nodded for Kay to go ahead of him. She gave him a brief wide-eyed look that said she was somewhat overwhelmed but not yet regretting her choice to come.

William quickly deposited the gifts in the middle of the room, and in the middle of a curious group of girls, so that his mom could give him a good hug. Annie and his dad had crowded into the room by the time she let go. William got a hug and a thump on the back from his dad and even a short hug from Annie "because it's Christmas."

Kay arranged her share of the presents more carefully than necessary. William was sure she was hedging to avoid the hug brigade. He figured opening the presents would be enough of a distraction to get her off the hook.

"The kids want to open the presents we brought, Mom."

"Of course they do." She smiled indulgently at her grandkids while waving off William's hint. "I haven't welcomed your friend yet. We're so glad you joined us, Kay."

"Thank you, Mrs. Dakley." Kay turned to Annie. "I do appreciate the invitation."

"Call me Diana."

Annie said, "I'm just sorry you couldn't bring those adorable babies this time."

"We heard you're letting the other grandparents have a turn with them and that makes us like you even more," Diana said.

William wondered if Kay noticed the inflection when his mom called her his friend and the suggestion of "other" grandparents. She wasn't exactly being subtle about her hopes for the future.

Kay smiled shyly at Diana. She gave up the show of organizing the gifts to stand and face everyone.

William's dad took the opportunity to swoop her into a bear

hug while Annie said, "Are you missing the boys terribly or trying to enjoy the reprieve from diapers?"

"Can we open the presents?" Ariana asked. She was holding one. Bailey had stopped waiting for permission to hand them out.

"Am I allowed to say both?" Kay moved towards Annie as she answered and away from William's parents.

His mom saw the hint and settled for patting Kay's arm.

"Of course," Annie said. "That's probably the only right answer."

"How's the job going at the church?" Diana asked.

"Great so far. I only put in two weeks before we closed up for Christmas."

The sound of tearing paper filled the room as Taylor got her hands on a present.

"I guess we're doing presents now," William said.

When no one stopped Taylor, the older girls began to rip into their presents.

Bailey had given Michael one. He was trying to open it while leaning against a wall. William judged that his brother was within five seconds of dropping the present, and he'd likely fall trying to pick it up. "That's going to be a lot easier sitting down." He took hold of Michael's elbow and guided him to a chair.

Michael allowed himself to be led, but he said, "I can do it."

"I know," William said. "I suspect you've been getting some practice. Did you get that hat today?"

The hat in question got knocked a bit sideways as Michael hit the chair. He dropped the present into his lap to straighten the hat. "I always wear this hat," he said.

"I see." William looked at his dad, who pointed to Jake and Annie to indicate they had given Michael the hat.

"Your presents are on the sofa." Bailey was looking at

William and pointing to a stack. She wasn't actually pointing at it so much as gesturing wildly for him to hurry up and get them open.

William made his way to the only seat left in the room, next to his mom. Jake was leaning against a wall and Kay, presumably having noticed that there were more people than chairs, was sitting on the floor in a corner with two presents on the carpet in front of her.

Diana Dakley tried to stop her son. "Be a gentleman and let Kay have the sofa. William can sit on the floor," she added to Kay.

"I'm fine here," Kay said. She seemed reluctant to give up her corner for the more comfortable place in the middle of the fray.

William got a look from his mom that said he'd be risking some serious disapproval if he took that seat after she warned him away from it. "Go on now," she said.

Kay wanted to stay where she was though. This was one time when not offering his seat felt like the more chivalrous choice, no matter how his mom saw it. He shifted the presents to draw attention to them as he sat. "The girls have already assigned me this place," he said, offering his mom a grandkid-related excuse.

She raised her eyebrows at him somewhat threateningly. She couldn't take away her 25-year-old's TV privileges, but it sure looked as though she wanted to.

"So what did you get there, Michael?" William asked, hoping to turn his mom's attention.

Michael was still fumbling with the package though. He hadn't even gotten the paper off. His coordination was about on par with his ability to distinguish truth from fantasy.

"Do you need a hand, son?" Cliff Dakley leaned forward in his chair.

Michael didn't appear to hear the offer. He was enjoying – and completely engrossed in – the struggle in front of him.

Cliff sat back. "Have you opened the one from us yet, Kay?" he called. "I'll take credit for picking it out if you like it."

Kay took the gift from the floor and peeled back the paper. William couldn't see what it was from where he sat. It seemed to be an article of clothing.

"Oh, it's pretty," Kay said.

"Don't you dare take credit for picking that out."

"I believe I offered an opinion."

"Thank you, Mrs. Dakley and Mr. Dakley," Kay said, using a neutral tone.

"Diana."

Cliff said, "I'll correct you when you can call me Dad." He gave a tiny guffaw, then looked at Jake, who still didn't call him Dad.

Kay winced as though the older man had just embarrassed himself. Jake might have been hoping for a place to hide. Diana sent her husband a look that suggested he might be about to be grounded, too. Annie couldn't contain her smirk even though all three girls were competing to show their mom what had been in their presents. And Michael kept trying to unwrap his present as though he was the only person in the room.

"How long did it take Michael to open that hat?" William said, because someone had to say something.

Annie apparently took pity on him. She moved the subject along. "I wrapped it special," she said with a wink. "No tape. Mom and Dad got him new gloves. He immediately put them on, and I was glad he'd already opened ours."

Michael finally got the wrapping free, and it fell to the floor. The lid was clear so he could see the belt buckle from Kay through the package. "Oh, it's like Gunsmoke," he said in an awed voice. "Marshal Dillon has this one."

144

"Is that so?" William asked.

Michael nodded while his dad shrugged.

Annie said, "You got him watching Gunsmoke now?"

"That's my job," Michael said.

"You work at the factory," Annie corrected.

"Yeah, yeah… I watch Gunsmoke at the factory."

Annie and William questioned their parents with their eyes. That *could* be true.

Diana shook her head. "You watch Gunsmoke with your father."

"Hey!" Michael's eyes widened with a new idea. "I'm going to ride a raft."

"A raft?" William didn't have to fake interest. "I'd like to hear about this raft."

Michael mirrored his brother's expectant expression. "Do you need help with those presents, William?"

Jake let out a laugh that he tried to cover with a cough. Annie shared a smile with her husband while William looked at Kay, whom he was pleased to see also fighting laughter. He was tempted to let Michael open his presents for him, but he didn't want to further distract him. "You said you were going on a raft. What raft?"

"A raft?" Michael's face came alive with a huge grin. "Did you get a raft for Christmas?"

"Open your presents, Uncle William." Bailey was suddenly right in front of him. "Everyone else is done."

William scanned the room. He was in fact the only one still holding unopened presents, though he didn't know how they had all managed to open theirs while he wasn't paying attention. Kay and Annie seemed to be talking about what they gave each other. His mom held up the scrapbooking supplies from William and thanked him. A hobby with consumables made her the easiest person to shop for. But her thanks reminded him that Kay's gift was still hidden. Should he just pull it out now and get it over with?

"What are you waiting for?" Now Ariana was standing at his side.

"Kay said we could do her hair after the presents," Bailey said. She was holding a basket of brightly colored bows and ribbons and jeweled clips.

Taylor closed in and ripped a chunk of paper off one insufficiently guarded present.

"I guess I'll open that one first," William said.

"Can I help, too?" Ariana grabbed for a present.

"Wait, wait." William gently took the half-opened one from the toddler as he asked for patience. He was holding one present from Kay, one from Annie and Jake, and one from his parents. "You can each open one for me, but you have to do it one at a time so I know who gave me what. Let's let Taylor finish first."

She had tiny pigtails that fell forward as she bent her head to concentrate. She tore the paper into scraps and kept ripping after a book dropped. William picked up a copy of *The Divine Comedy*.

"You said recently you'd been meaning to read that for some time."

William nodded at Kay. "I remember. Thanks for taking away my excuse."

She smiled at the sarcasm.

"I can't promise it'll be soon, but I will read this eventually. Thank you."

"I'm next." Ariana held a present up for William to see the tag.

"Who's taking the tour with me this afternoon?" Cliff clapped his hands and began to rub them together. His eyes eagerly scanned the room like a cartoon villain overseeing his sinister plot. Though William may not have made that comparison if he had been less familiar with "the tour."

"I'll pass, Dad," he said.

Diana touched his arm. "You'd pass on time with your parents?"

"Driving around aimlessly is not what I'd call quality time."

"It's not aimless," Diana said. Her tone wasn't fully convincing.

"You want to go for a drive, Michael?" Cliff tried to get interest from his other son.

It was Taylor who answered. "I want to go! I want to go!"

Jake looked at Annie for one of those wordless married people conversations before he said, "Is it all right if I drive then so we don't have to move her car seat?"

"The more the merrier." Cliff put one arm around his youngest grandchild and held out the other to Michael. "Come on, Michael. You want to join us on the tour, Kay?"

Kay looked up at the sound of her name. "I'm sorry," she said. "I already have an appointment to get my hair done." The older girls were lining up supplies next to her. She met William's eyes long enough to share a secret smile at her easy excuse. Kay knew about the tour, or at least William's version of the tour.

It had been his parents' favorite pastime when he was growing up. Every few weeks or so, his parents would drag all three kids into the car for the tour. It seemed like hours and hours of "There's where I lived when my parents first moved us here," "I was riding down that hill when I fell from my bike and broke my arm," and "The first time I ever went to a birthday party, the kid lived in that house." The worst part, in William's opinion, were the sites on the tour that weren't even there anymore. "Our wedding reception was in a building that was right there before they tore it down." "The park had a merry-go-round right over there that I loved when I was a kid."

"Wouldn't it be better to go at night when the Christmas lights are on?" Annie asked, drawing William's attention back to the current iteration of the tour.

"We see plenty of Christmas lights in Cleveland," Diana said. "Trips down memory lane are better with daylight."

"Well, I guess I need to stay and work on dinner." Annie didn't even try to make her disappointment sound genuine.

William watched the group break into those going and those staying as he realized that he had missed opening his own presents as well. Annie and Jake had given him a cookbook, most likely his sister's idea of a joke. "Very funny," he said, holding it up for Annie.

She smiled as though it was funny. "Well, if I gave it to Kay, it'd really be a gift for you."

William thought about that as he looked at the mouth-watering dish on the cover. Sometimes Kay had dinner ready about the time he came home from work. Other times he was able to help, even if that usually only meant holding a baby. Being in the kitchen with Kay and Pete and Will was regularly his favorite time of day. Maybe this actually was a good present. "Do you think you'd be willing to try some of these?"

"Definitely," Kay said. "I could use some new ideas. Can I take a look?"

He set the book on the floor and slid it across the carpet to her, still thinking of helping her cook. The memory was embellished with William providing real help and Kay accepting it by standing much closer to him.

When he woke up from his daydream, Annie had disappeared

into the kitchen. Christmas music was coming from that room. Kay was slowly turning the pages of the cookbook with an occasional wince. Bailey and Ariana were apparently not the most gentle hairdressers. They were full of compliments though. Kay's hair was so pretty, so shiny, so soft.

William's fingers began to itch with the desire to join his nieces. He really wanted to be the one running his hands through her hair, which meant he really needed to leave the room before he did something foolish. "I'm going to make sure Annie is making something good for dinner."

No one looked up as he left. Kay acknowledged his departure with half a smile.

Annie was standing over the sink surrounded by a cloud of steam. Then she lifted what appeared to be a heavy pot to the opposite counter.

"What's that?" William asked.

"Sweet potatoes." She removed a slotted lid and began to poke into the pan with a whisk. "It's a little early to get them into the oven. I'm just going to get them mashed up and ready for now."

William nodded as though he had any idea what she was talking about. He watched her hand go up and down. The sweet potatoes were likely too soft to be therapeutic. He could imagine mashing something harder though. The churning motion made him think of beating, smashing, pulverizing.

"William?"

"Huh?"

"You look like you're about to take my head off, and I haven't done anything."

"Oh." He tried to shake off the feelings of frustration. It was Christmas after all. "Sorry."

"You okay?"

He did not want to talk about it. "You're not gonna put marshmallows on those, are you?"

Annie snorted and otherwise ignored his question. "Come on," she said. She put down the whisk and walked towards the quiet room. "I need to let those cool a bit before I add the eggs anyway."

It appeared that Annie expected William to follow her. She went around the corner and her feet showed through the doorway as she sat on a beanbag. William was not going to talk to her about Kay this time. Annie had a knack for getting him to spill his guts, but it wouldn't work today. He went into the quiet room and lowered himself onto the other beanbag chair. His knees came up like a shield.

"How's Kay doing? Her sister must be in her thoughts a lot at Christmas."

"I think... she's managing. We went to the cemetery before we came here."

Annie nodded. "Her dad's coming next week?"

"On the third. I hope... I hope it goes okay." William was probably far more nervous about the visit than Kay was. People grieved in different ways, but Mr. Donovan grieved angry. The last time he was in town, he'd looked as though he wanted to throw something when Beth's name came up. This would be the first visit since Kay moved in with William, which might put him in the middle of something.

"It sounds like Kay enjoys working with Mrs. Adams," Annie said. "It's awesome that she can bring Pete."

"I think that was the clincher when she was deciding whether or not to take the job. Of course, he's gotten to where he can almost scooch himself in a deliberate direction. Crawling may not be more than a month or so away." Kay was only allowed to bring the baby to work until he could crawl.

"Still... a little extra time probably helps her adjust. How much longer until you ask her to marry you?"

William just glared at Annie.

"That is still your eventual hope, isn't it?" she asked, her tone casual and immune to the glare.

"Years and years at this rate," William said. "I went and shot myself in the foot without even knowing it."

"What do you mean?"

"I can't even ask her out now that... she's kind of stuck until... the church isn't paying enough for her to afford rent somewhere else and if I...there'd be pressure..." The situation was difficult to put into words.

"I see," Annie said, still way too calm and peaceful. "You mean that now she's financially dependent on you, it'd be sort of like hitting on an employee."

Maybe it wasn't difficult for other people to put into words. "Yes," William said. "Something like that."

"Hmm." Annie nodded thoughtfully. She looked annoyingly unsurprised by the idea.

"Don't tell me you saw this coming."

"I said having her move in might cause you some problems."

"You didn't elaborate," William said. "I assumed you were mostly talking about... Why didn't you tell me?"

She smiled. "You didn't want me to tell you. Nothing would have stopped you from suggesting it because you were freaking out about her moving to Seattle. If I had told you this would happen, we'd be having this same conversation with a big fat I told you so in the air."

William got the distinct impression that there was still a big fat I told you so in the air without anyone having actually told him so. It rankled him into asking for advice he didn't want to give Annie the satisfaction of asking for. "So what am I supposed to do now? Wait forever for her to move out just to start working on getting her to move in for real?"

"Does for real mean with a ring?"

He tried another glare. Annie knew what he meant and she'd gotten him to say too much already.

Annie tipped her head and her expression became more compassionate, which was actually worse than gloating. "I think you need to talk to her. There's a lot of wiggle room between hitting on someone and telling her how you feel about her."

"I hate your advice."

"Just because it might be hard doesn't make it bad advice. By the way, what happened to her present?"

"Oh, yeah. Do you think she noticed she didn't get something from me?"

"*I* noticed. I just thought you exchanged presents before you came over until you opened one from her."

"It's in my coat pocket," William said. He paused to glance around the corner, something he should have done a few other times during the conversation. "I got her a necklace with both the boys' birthstones. It's, like, a mom thing. But it has a heart. I was afraid if she opened a heart in front of certain people there would be enough teasing to embarrass her."

Annie pinched her lips in a guilty expression, though the certain people he meant were their parents.

"Of course, now I need to figure out how to explain when we get home. If she thinks I'd be embarrassed about giving her a heart—"

"It might prompt a discussion you need to have," Annie finished.

William was not going to have whatever discussion Annie had in mind, not today, not when Kay had so many other things on her mind.

Annie appeared to read that on his face. She rolled her eyes and said, "Just give it to her right now. Mom and Dad aren't here to say anything. You can tell her you forgot to get it out in the earlier chaos."

There was some truth to that excuse. William got to his feet quickly. "Okay. That advice isn't awful."

13

She had to admit he was crawling. As long as he was dragging along on his tummy or moving slowly, she could say he was "learning to crawl." Kay watched Pete move across the carpet after his brother and knew it wouldn't be fair to keep him on her lap at work any longer. She would talk to Louise about leaving Pete starting on Monday.

Mrs. Adams had a lot of connections. When she found out that Kay was leaving Will at a day care center twenty miles away, she insisted on helping her find a better situation. She had a great option within a few phone calls.

Louise had been a nanny for many years. She was a little over sixty when her last family outgrew her and thought perhaps it was time to retire. After a few months off, she was missing kids. Mrs. Adams had done little talking to convince her that Kay's part-time need was a perfect semi-retirement compromise. And she lived right around the corner from the church, which was perfect for Kay as well.

The stew Kay was making for dinner smelled wonderful. She gave it a stir, then put her elbow on the counter to watch her boys play. William's house had been sparsely furnished and since she didn't have much either, they were able to mostly fit everything in his house. Except that they didn't need two kitchen tables. Both were small four-person tables, which was all they needed. Both were old, second-hand tables. They'd decided to use Kay's because the bottom of one of the legs on William's was splintered, and he was afraid Will would hurt himself on it. That table had sat in the garage until a week ago.

William got the idea to cut off the splintered half of the leg and the other three to match. That left it a little over two feet high. He thought Will could drive cars or trains on it. So far, Will preferred to drive himself on it. He liked to pull himself onto the table, slide along on his tummy, then slip his legs off another side.

Right now, Pete was crawling – slightly jerky movements, but definitely crawling – under the table. Will was sliding around on the top peeking over the sides. Each time he spotted his brother, they both erupted in giggles. Kay thought it was the most beautiful thing God had ever put in front of her. "Do you see them, too, Beth?" she whispered.

Her heart ached that her sister couldn't be standing right next to her to watch them, but it remained in one piece. It didn't hurt so much that she couldn't laugh at the adorable antics. Will backed up, spun himself around and looked over the opposite side. Pete took a bit longer to get turned around. The giggles started again as soon as they found each other.

Under their joy came another happy sound, a key turning in a lock. William was home. Kay waved him towards her as soon as he got through the door. Then she nodded at Will and Pete.

William smiled as they broke into another round of cute laughs. "How long have they been doing that?" He spoke softly so as not to disrupt the game.

Kay shrugged. "Probably not more than a few minutes. Aren't they cute?"

William barely nodded because of how intently he was watching, but the way he was watching answered the question even better. He was enthralled. It was plain that he was watching two boys he cared about very strongly. It was even possible that he loved them as much as Kay did.

The thought swam around in her head for a while. It felt like a good thing. It wasn't a burden to have the boys living with him if he loved them, yet some instinct was trying to push the thought away as though it was unsettling.

"It smells good in here," William said. He was eyeing the pot on the stove with an implied question.

"Beef stew," Kay said. "And I thought you could make some biscuits to go with it."

"You thought *I* could make biscuits? Are you feeling all right? Have there been any other hallucinations?"

Kay knew his reaction would be something like that. She laughed anyway, then plowed ahead with the lesson. "I got a mix," she said. "All you have to do is add milk and put them in the oven."

"You try to make it sound easy by leaving out a lot of steps. I'm betting I also need to turn on the oven and put them on a pan and grease it first and—"

"It sounds to me like you already know an awful lot about this." Kay cut him off and enjoyed the look on his face while he tried to go from listing all the steps to acting as though he didn't know the first thing about any of it.

"Okay, so I know the oven has to be hot, but I don't know how hot."

"Lucky for you, instructions are on the box." Kay set the box on the counter in front of him and got a bowl down as well. "I'll supervise."

"Are you going to supervise like you supervised the cookies?" He smiled ingratiatingly.

Kay shook her head like she might if Will was reaching for something he shouldn't have. Her first attempt at teaching William to cook had been chocolate chip cookies. She thought getting to eat them would be good enticement. But after cleaning out the microwave when he "softened" the butter into a puddle with nothing under it and picking eggshells out of the bowl and barely stopping the wet spoon from dipping into the flour, she'd pushed William aside. Kay hadn't realized how thoroughly she'd taken over until the cookies came out of the oven. William had been giving her a hard time ever since.

"I'm going to let you do it," Kay said. "I won't say anything unless it looks like something catastrophic is about to happen." She took a little step back to illustrate her intention.

William tried to give everything in the kitchen a doubtful scowl – including Kay – but it was ruined by the smile that broke free as another wave of baby giggles rose in the room. "All right, let's give this a try." He pushed up his sleeves and turned to the sink to wash his hands. Then he tipped the mix box back to read the instructions.

Kay tried to be patient. Reading slowly was not catastrophic. Even when it seemed as though he was just staring at the box to waste time. Finally, he sent her a sheepish look. "I'm stuck already. This has three different recipes."

"Make the smallest one."

"Will that be enough for leftovers?" He'd regularly been packing leftovers for work lunches.

"I think so," Kay said.

He nodded, then went back to studying the box.

Kay checked on the boys. Will was still scooting himself around the short table. Pete had crawled out from under it though. Their game was over. The tag on a stuffed animal had gotten Pete's attention, and it was getting a very close inspection. She didn't know how long either activity would distract the boys from dinnertime so she ladled out a bowl of stew to cool.

William was still holding the biscuit box with his eyes glued to the back of it. She didn't know if he was trying to memorize the instructions or hoping she'd take over if he was slow enough. His fingers eventually ripped open the top of the package, crookedly. His eyes darted to Kay at the same time. "I might actually be able to do this."

She smiled at the shaky confidence. She wanted him to enjoy a challenge, not feel as though she was pushing him to do some of her share of the work. She was supposed to be doing the bulk of the housework in exchange for free rent. It didn't count as work if they had fun together.

William measured and added the mix and the milk. He pulled a regular – more appropriate for eating cereal – spoon from a drawer and began to stir. He had to grip the end to keep his fingers out of the dough. He didn't seem to mind so Kay didn't tell him which spoon he should be using. She did have to speak up when he was about to spoon the first one onto the pan. "Wait," she said. "Grease the pan."

"Oh, yeah." He looked grateful for the help rather than annoyed at interference.

By the time the biscuits came out of the oven, William had cleaned up the kitchen and Kay had Will in his high chair and Pete in her lap. She was holding a bottle for Pete in one hand and had the other one ready in case Will got any ideas about tossing his bowl of stew onto the floor. So far, he seemed to be enjoying the food. She'd strained out most of the broth to make it less messy.

It was probably time to buy a second high chair. Kay hadn't yet found a good used one. Pete was usually only having a few bites at each meal. He sat in Will's chair when he was done. But he was showing more and more interest in what everyone else was eating. Kay eventually wanted all four of them to sit around the table at the same time. Sort of like a family.

Another thought that was quickly banished from her mind as weirdly uncomfortable.

William brought over two adult bowls of stew and a plate of biscuits. They said a quick prayer and began to eat. William was quietly thinking about something. The biscuits were different sizes and the smaller ones were a bit dark on the bottoms. Kay wondered if he was working out how to fix that next time.

He was evidently thinking of something entirely different because he said, "What would you think about taking Will and Pete to the zoo?"

"The zoo?" Kay didn't know what she thought about the out of the blue suggestion. She put her spoon down.

Will took advantage of her distraction to dump his bowl onto his tray, which was at least better than the floor. She handed him a biscuit to buy herself a few more minutes before she had to clean him up. He opened wide and smashed it against his face.

"Do you mean the Toledo Zoo or the one in Cleveland?" Either was at least an hour away.

"I was thinking Cleveland because we could stop in and visit my parents. Maybe Michael, too."

Kay nodded, though she still didn't entirely understand. "It's February," she said. Zoos were mostly outdoors. William couldn't be imagining wandering around in the snow for hours with two babies.

"It'll be March next week, which means it's almost spring. I thought we might have some warmish days around the corner and you'd probably want some time to think about what Will and Pete would need for a day trip so you could think about that while we sort of… keep an eye on the forecast the next few weekends." William poked his spoon at his dinner. He appeared self-conscience at the poor reception his idea was getting. "If that's something you'd even want to do."

"Hmm." Kay felt bad for dismissing the idea before she gave it any real thought. She hadn't been to a zoo since she was a kid. The boys might be too young to appreciate the animals, but just being exposed to some new scenery could be a good experience for them. As long as it wasn't too cold. "I guess we might be able to try a trip to the zoo."

~~~~

It was the first week of April before the weather cooperated enough for the day trip. They'd planned it out as more of a half-day trip. They left after an early lunch so the boys could nap during the drive. That worked so well that both boys were sound asleep when they arrived to pick up Michael, who they'd decided might like to come to the zoo as well.

"Do you want to wait with the babies so we don't have to wake them up?" William asked.

"That might be best."

"Are you sure? It might take a while." William rolled his eyes in a here-we-go-again sort of way. "I'm betting he's surprised to see me."

"It might take me just as long to figure out how I'm going to get between those car seats."

"I can ride in the back."

Kay shook her head at the offer. "I'm smaller than you are."

"All right." William looked doubtfully between the car and

161

the group home. "I'll be as fast as I can." Then he jogged to the front steps.

There was also a ramp down the side. Michael lived with five other residents, individuals with various disabilities. There was always at least one staff member present who coordinated chores, passed out medication, mediated disputes and so on. Michael had moved in shortly after he finished high school. His parents moved nearby around the same time, which was only a month or two before Kay met William. Since she'd only known his parents to be living in Cleveland, she had to keep reminding herself that it was a recent change for William.

Then again, maybe it wasn't so recent anymore. When she tried to think about first getting to know William, it felt like a long time ago. That scared her. Thinking about meeting William made her think about not knowing him anymore, at least not having him close. She didn't want to think about that. It made her want to concentrate hard on the task at hand.

There was no way she could climb over or under either baby to the middle seat without waking one up or getting herself stuck. If she took out Pete's car seat to get in, she didn't think she could bring it in after her without serious jostling. It appeared her best option was to climb from the front seat to the back seat.

Kay began to question her judgment when her face was pressed against the back of the seat and her legs didn't fit past the front. She twisted a bit to get one leg around the back of the passenger seat but couldn't balance enough to pull the other leg through without grabbing one of the car seats she was trying not to shake. Five minutes later, she was sitting between Pete and Will without a clear description of how she'd managed it, nor why a section of her lower lip felt puffy.

Kay touched her finger to that sore spot as William exited the house. He held the door for Michael and appeared to steer him towards the ramp. Michael grabbed the railing to proceed down the steps. William didn't lower his arms until they were safely at the bottom.

Michael moseyed to the car wearing the white cowboy hat he'd had on at Christmas and a belt buckle even larger than the one Kay gave him. William helped him into the car and instructed him to buckle up. Though they reached up at the same time, Michael's lack of coordination and Kay's lack of space made it a race between the tortoise and the tortoise.

William walked around the car, buckled himself, then started the car. "You ready?" His eyes darted between Michael and Kay and took in the fact that neither was ready.

"The buckle is wedged under Pete's car seat," Kay muttered, trying to cram her fingers into the same tiny space to tug it free.

A zip and a smack sounded as Michael's seat belt slipped from his hand and back to the starting line.

Kay freed her buckle and connected the belt. Then she smoothed it over her lap. A car seat was digging into her hip bone on one side and left her no place to put her arm on the other. Fortunately, the zoo wasn't more than fifteen minutes from Michael's house, once they got moving.

The pace was slow at the zoo as well. Michael walked slowly. Kay was pushing a double stroller. William alternated between picking up toys the babies tossed overboard and grabbing Michael's arm to keep him on his feet when he stumbled. Plus, Michael was fascinated by the benches. He wanted to sit on each one simply because it was there. None of them were in a hurry though.

Kay enjoyed some of the animals. What she noticed most, however, were all the families she saw. And the way they smiled at her as though she was one of them. People who heard her using names probably assumed Will was even named after William, a junior.

Her mind continued to focus on families as they met Mr. and Mrs. Dakley for dinner after the zoo. She saw them as a team, appreciated the way they cared for each other and their grown boys. It was evident in every gesture and smile.

Will and Pete fell asleep again on the drive home. Kay didn't even realize she was drifting off until she woke up when the car stopped.

William whispered, "I'll get the boys," as the sleep fog cleared from Kay's brain.

A blast of chilled air woke her more fully when she opened her door. The day had been pleasant for walking but was much cooler now that the sun had set.

William had Will lying against his shoulder. He used the other hand to open the door on Pete's side.

"I got this one," Kay said.

He nodded and grabbed the diaper bag for her.

Kay gently lifted Pete's carrier and followed William into his very quiet house, where he was standing uncertainly in the hallway.

"Do you mind if I put him in the crib?" William asked. His voice was low to keep from waking the little guy.

Kay motioned for him to lead the way. William hadn't come into the room she shared with the boys since he helped them move in, yet sending him that way now didn't feel momentous. He gently placed Will in his crib, then slipped his shoes off. Kay leaned over the next crib to put Pete down as well.

The two adults stepped softly and slowly away from the cribs. Kay's eyes went past William to her bedside table. Her laptop was sitting there on top of several scribble-covered papers that were her budget calculations. She'd recorded every income and expense in the four plus months that she'd been living in William's house. She was trying to figure out exactly how much she needed to earn to live on her own and how much she'd owe him when she moved out and how long it might take to actually move out. It was all very complicated.

"Did you have fun today?" William whispered.

She nodded without even thinking. Fun probably wasn't the right word. The drive had been long, the stroller was a hassle, keeping both boys quiet in the restaurant had been a challenge, and the whole day wore her out. Even though it was only a half-day in theory. She'd still enjoyed it. There was no question.

"Good." William smiled. "I'm glad it wasn't a terrible idea. See you in the morning." He turned and walked out of the room.

"Good night," Kay said to his back. She closed the door to get herself ready for bed. The papers on the table kept calling her attention though. Finally, she closed her eyes and admitted what she'd been refusing to admit for a long time. She was making that budget complicated on purpose. She was trying to justify her temporary situation because she didn't want it to be temporary.

14

"I think something is wrong," William said. And he meant something other than the fact that he was talking to his sister about something he didn't want to talk to her about. Again.

Annie stopped pretending to straighten the kids' books with her free hand. She was holding Pete in her other arm. "Wrong how?" she asked.

"I don't know. She's quiet."

"Quiet how?"

"Like... distracted."

Annie opened her mouth.

William said, "If you say, 'distracted how?' I'm going to leave the room." He'd only come into the quiet room to put away a few books for Taylor. Annie had popped in at the same time with a barrage of seemingly innocuous questions. Now he was having a conversation he hadn't intended to have. That made him a little cranky.

Annie glanced at Pete and almost managed to look as though her smile was aimed at him instead of her frustrated brother. "What makes you think she's distracted?"

"I catch her staring into space a lot and on Sunday... We've been doing a board game after church, and she actually said she didn't have the concentration for that at the moment. She's especially quiet if the boys are napping or we're otherwise alone. It feels like there's something on her mind that she doesn't want to tell me about."

"Hmm. Doesn't that also describe you?"

"No." They weren't talking about him. At least not directly. And he was sure he hid it better anyway. "This is different. It's sudden. It's… I'm afraid it's my fault."

Annie raised her eyebrows dramatically. "What did you do?"

He wanted to defend himself, insist he hadn't done anything. And he hadn't done anything inappropriate or offensive. But he wasn't totally innocent either. He'd been gradually giving himself away. Kay always braided her hair before bed. In the mornings, she'd just pull out the rubber band and let it come undone on its own. William had gotten in the habit of giving unnecessary help. He combed his fingers through her hair under the guise of speeding the unbraiding when he only wanted an excuse to touch it. He hung out in the kitchen when she had dinner fully under control. Not only did he not correct them, but he knew he looked way too happy when people at church complimented his "beautiful family." And of course he was the one who insisted she take a job that wouldn't allow her to move out. "I don't think it was any one thing," he said. "I think she's just finally putting everything together."

"Put what together?" The voice was not Annie's but came from a smaller person who resembled Annie.

The quiet room in an otherwise busy house was not a great place for a private conversation. William looked at Ariana and tried to be grateful it wasn't Kay standing in the doorway.

Ariana raised her eyebrows at him much the same way his sister had a minute earlier. "Did you break something?" she asked.

"Not yet." William lunged for her.

She squealed and tried to run but wasn't fast enough.

He picked her up and held her flailing legs in the air. "Where should I drop you?" he asked.

"Nowhere! Nowhere!" she gasped between laughs.

"I bet I can find a good place." William carried her through the kitchen and into the living room. The screaming child caused a lot of heads to turn their way as he entered. He scanned the room and found an empty spot on the sofa. He lifted Ariana higher as he got closer but only actually dropped her about a foot above the cushion.

She jumped up already asking him to do it again. But Taylor and Will were both at his feet with their arms raised yelling, "Me next! Me next!"

William scooped up Taylor, swung her around, then dropped her gently to the sofa before he gave Will a turn. All three of them got a second turn. "All right," he said. "That's enough. I've dropped you all enough."

"Not me!" Bailey was standing nearby looking eager to be picked up.

"You might be too big," William told her. "I think I can only carry people who are five or younger."

"I'm *six*," Ariana corrected.

"Oh, yeah." She'd had a birthday the previous month. It was only a few days after his own so it should have been the one he could remember. "Six or younger," he said.

Bailey's eyebrows went up in an annoyingly familiar expression. "That's not true," she said. "You picked me and Ariana up at the same time last week."

"You've gotten bigger since then. And I've gotten older."

The opposing forehead scrunched tighter.

William wiped the accusation from her face by picking her up and tossing her onto the sofa, gently of course but maybe not as gently as the younger kids.

There was a loud sigh from behind him. Annie said, "Why do you insist on winding the girls up before you leave?"

"So they'll miss me until next week as much as you do."

Annie snorted in response. "I'll miss this little guy anyway." She snuggled Pete briefly before she put him down. "He doesn't let me hold him as much now that he's mobile though. They never stay babies very long."

Kay held up Pete's jacket and he crawled to her to let her put it on him. Then she handed the younger boy to William while she gathered Will and the diaper bag. Kay said her goodbyes and was out the door first. William looked back as Annie closed the door behind them. Her mouth formed the words "tell her."

He waved as though he didn't notice the message. He prayed on the subject often and felt sure that God was telling him to wait, that everything would work out exactly the way he wanted between him and Kay if he was willing to wait long enough.

The sudden change in Kay had him worried that he was wrong, that his optimism was founded in denial rather than hope. Maybe it wasn't God that convinced him to wait. Maybe it was fear. Maybe Kay had realized he wanted more than she could give and was close to telling him to stop holding his breath.

She wouldn't say it like that though. She was too nice. That was probably why she seemed distracted. She couldn't figure out a nice way to tell him to stop holding his breath for something that would never happen.

Kay put the boys to bed, then got in the shower to get herself ready while William flipped through the channels on the TV. Even sports highlights weren't taking his mind off the fact that Kay might be days or even minutes from giving him some bad news.

She came into the room in a plaid nightgown braiding her hair over her shoulder. She sat on the opposite end of the sofa looking nervous. Distracted and nervous. It was coming.

William switched off the TV. He took a cue from Annie, though he wouldn't tell her that, and tried to ease into a talk with something casual. "Taylor sure had you reading a lot of books tonight."

"Yeah. I keep trying to read with Will, and he runs off two pages into anything. It was nice to read with someone with an actual attention span."

"Dinner was good," William said.

Kay nodded. "Annie spoils us."

Too late, William noticed his possible blunder and tried to recover. "Dinner is good when you cook, too."

She smiled a little as though she realized he was squirming. But it faded quickly. Something was definitely wrong.

William resolved to ask what it was. He reached inside for a glimmer of hope that it had nothing to do with him after all. He held tight to the idea that it could even be something he could fix. "Is something on your mind?" he asked.

Kay tipped her head to the side with a frown. It wasn't a nod, but it was confirmation. She didn't say anything.

He didn't press her, just waited to see if she was willing to share. Meanwhile, he began to fantasize that whatever it was only needed a hug to solve. He could pull her close and promise not to let go until... he just wouldn't let go.

Kay opened her mouth. A wordless breath was the only thing that came out.

William might have asked again if she wanted to talk about something, but thinking about holding her had given rise to thoughts he wasn't supposed to be having, and he was preoccupied with wrestling those thoughts back into submission.

"Sometimes I wish we were married."

Kay was the one who said it. William needed a few seconds

to process the fact that words from his head had come out of Kay's mouth. He was pretty sure she wasn't sharing any of his other thoughts, but if she had a thread that somehow ended with them married, he wanted to hear details. "Uh…" He cleared his throat to say something more coherent. He said, "What?"

Which wasn't really more coherent.

~~~~

Kay took a deep breath and tried to pretend she hadn't said anything out loud. Maybe William hadn't even heard her. She glanced his way. He looked sort of like the time he'd put his knee down on the corner of a block and was trying not to yell in front of the babies. It seemed unlikely he would let her get away with pretending she hadn't said something.

Her thoughts had been racing the last few days. She intended to keep those thoughts on the interior track until they slowed enough to steer. Now she had to keep talking because her comment needed some attempt at explanation. "I've been thinking a lot lately," she said. Just not about what she wanted to say to William, unfortunately. "For a long time now, I've… I've been refusing to look ahead at all. And it hasn't been a good savoring the moment kind of mentality. It's more like a who cares if there's consequences as long as it gets me through today kind of thinking."

"You've been in crisis mode."

"Maybe." She was glad William seemed to recognize that she hadn't intentionally been selfish. "But I think I've recovered enough that I'm no longer afraid to look at the future and think about… to try to plan what it should look like." And the more she thought about the future, the more she wished she could go back in time, not just to before she'd started this increasingly awkward conversation but all the way to when William asked her out. If she'd made a different impression, if they'd started dating instead of becoming friends, they might have been married – or at least on the way to married – when she gained custody of two babies.

How much easier would it have been if they'd been partners from the beginning? Now he was attached to the boys and not to her. That was the biggest problem. Overall. The biggest problem at the moment was trying to explain a lot of jumbled thoughts without sounding like she was trying to propose. "I think what has surprised me the most is that despite all the changes, nothing has changed."

William added confusion to his expression. Since he already looked concerned about what she was saying and desperate to say something himself, she felt sorry for him and tried to explain faster.

"I've always wanted to get married and raise a family. It's... I think of it like a vocation, what I'm called to do with my life. And I still want that. I've been thinking about my chances of... well, there aren't any single guys where I work and I'm not going to meet anyone at your sister's house, which is my entire social life. So I'd have to be deliberate... join a group at church or go online and... you know how I am, how long it takes me to even consider someone a friend. I'm thinking realistically, and with some optimism, at least five years before I can find someone and spend enough time with him – given my time at work and with the boys – before there's someone I'm ready to marry. I know that five years out of my life, in the course of everything, isn't that big... but it's a significant chunk of their childhood." Kay paused and pointed to the wall where Will and Pete were sleeping on the other side.

"I don't want to screw this up," she said. "When I think about what I have to do... what I have to give up. Right now I have a job that I like. I like working at the church way more than I ever liked Timmond's. And because it's part time, I get to spend a lot of time with the boys. You're here to back me up with an extra set of hands and a break now and then from the constant attention they need. I have to quit the job I like for one I'll probably like less. Louise doesn't want to go back to forty hours or more a week so I have to give up a sweet nanny for a situation that couldn't possibly be better. I have to move out on my own, put myself out there to meet a guy that I have no guarantee of meeting. I have to give up everything and go through a lot of struggle and heartache to get *a chance* at something that looks a lot like what I have right now." Only not as good. She and William couldn't go back to their old friendship after she'd been dreaming of marrying him. Whatever future she managed would include sad memories of him.

"You don't... uh..." William might have had as many competing thoughts as Kay because he seemed to be suffering for words and that was unusual for him. "You can stay longer," he said finally.

"But the longer I stay here..." Kay glanced towards the wall again, imagining the cribs on the other side and the precious contents. "The longer *we* stay, the more difficult this becomes. None of it is just about me. The four of us, we look like a family. When we go out, people don't see the mess I've made. They see a family. I'm afraid that's what Will and Pete see, even if they're too young to fully understand it. They've become attached to you. When we move out, it'll be like a divorce to them, after they've already lost their parents once. I hate doing that to them and to..." She looked at William. He wasn't telling her they could stay because he wanted to be nice. He wanted them to stay. "To you," she finished. "I know you love them. I feel like... with my neediness... that I've made you love them. And I'm going to repay everything you've done for us by taking them away. That's why I can't help but wish..."

William put his hand over his face. It seemed he didn't want to face the reality she painted any more than Kay did.

She liked the fantasy, the fantasy where William loved her, too. He did of course, just not in the way that could make them a real family. And it was annoying that thinking he had no desire to kiss her only made her picture the opposite. The fantasy made her face hot, and it made her want to be alone. "If things were different between us... well, I'm just saying that would be easier." Kay stood up. She really needed to get out of this room where she was embarrassing herself. "I was just thinking out loud and I'm sorry... sorry."

William opened his mouth like he wanted to stop her. He got up, too.

Kay was certain she'd done enough damage for one evening. She shook her head as she walked away, refusing to continue the conversation. Safe behind her bedroom door, she let the full picture enter her imagination. She wanted to marry William. Not only for the boys' sake or because it would be convenient. When she looked at the future, she wanted William to be her husband.

15

William didn't get much work done. At least not done well or efficiently. He'd been thinking that Kay was distracted and now that he knew why, he'd never been more accurately described by the word. He had two coworkers ask where his head was because it wasn't at work. Fortunately, he'd been there long enough that his reputation covered for him. The people who asked were concerned rather than irritated. Unfortunately, he didn't want his coworkers to be concerned about him either. That would likely invite questions about his personal life, which he did not discuss at work.

Even Chris had figured that out. After helping Kay move, he started asking how things were going with her. A few brief answers had convinced him to stop fishing.

There was a stack of paperwork waiting to be conquered. William let himself imagine the worst disaster he could manage with that workload. That was the mental shake he needed. He got through the rest of the workday without questions.

Only once he was driving home did he let himself resume thinking about Kay and what she'd said the previous night. She'd said a lot, maybe more than she'd ever shared in one sitting before, so he had a lot to think about.

William didn't go straight home. He pulled into a parking lot on the way and sat there replaying the evening. One comment stood out above all the others. "If things were different between us…"

It brought up a very important question. *Could* things be

different between them? Did Kay want that to happen? Would it help to keep talking about the possibility? Had he been patient long enough? Was it time to act? Act how? Talk first? It brought up many, many questions. He was going to go home and talk to Kay. About what exactly, he wasn't sure. But they definitely needed to keep talking. William shifted back into drive.

The house smelled great when he opened the door. Fresh bread? There was a homemade pizza crust on the counter, only half covered with sauce and a cutting board filled with chopped peppers in red, green and yellow.

His eyes went past the abandoned dinner prep to locate Kay in the next room. She was holding Will, who was calm but had traces of tears on his cheeks. He wiggled to be put down when he saw William. Pete was crawling towards William, but Will ran and got there first. He grabbed William's pant legs as though he intended to climb up. Pete stopped halfway and started crying for not getting there first.

Kay sighed and picked up Pete as William picked up Will. "We're not having a wonderful afternoon," she said.

"This looks awesome." William nodded to the pizza.

"It's not finished."

"And already I can tell it will be delicious."

"It may never be finished at the rate we're going," Kay said.

"All right. Let me see if us guys can stay out of your way for a bit." He reached out an arm to take Pete off her hands.

"Thank you. I'm glad you're home." She surveyed the scene, presumably to figure out where she'd left off. "Actually, you're kind of late, aren't you?"

"Umm..." William was surprised that she'd noticed, but a glance at the time told him he'd sat in that parking lot much longer than he'd thought. "I guess I am a little late."

"Play trucks," Will said, tugging on the front of William's shirt to get his attention.

William nodded approval of the idea and the timing of it. He carried the boys to the short table hoping no one would ask why he was late. He set them both down and spread the city. He'd bought a plain vinyl tablecloth and drew roads on it. Kay had helped him add some buildings and a playground. He brought over the box of cars and trucks and handed one to Pete, who sat and banged it against the leg of the table. Even Will wasn't really old enough to understand the concept of keeping the vehicles on the roads. He ran back and forth on one side of the table with a small garbage truck, his favorite, making sound effects.

William tried to model some pretend play by driving his car – on the road – to the school to pick up imaginary children. Someday soon Pete and Will would play more interactively. Would they still be living in this house when they were that old? William parked his toy car at the playground and looked at Kay working in the kitchen.

There was a lot riding on their next conversation. Or maybe the next few conversations. William sensed that he was on the verge of either gaining a family or losing one. His life would be profoundly affected no matter what.

"Twenty minutes," Kay announced from the kitchen as she closed the oven. She put something in the refrigerator, then came into the living room.

Pete had a car in his mouth. Kay gently pulled down the hand holding it to reveal a smile. She stood him up and turned him to face the table. He patted the surface with both hands while she supported him with one. His legs were strong but his balance needed the assist.

Kay put a car in front of Pete and pushed it back and forth to get his attention. It seemed that she was deliberately keeping her attention on the car as well.

Amanda Hamm

If she was already self-conscious about what she'd shared the night before, William figured there was no reason he shouldn't dive back in. He tried to keep the tone light. "Some of what you said last night... uh... it almost sounded like you'd be willing to marry me just so you don't have to look for someone else."

Kay's eyes popped up to his for a second before she refocused on the little car and crashed it into Pete's hand. He laughed and waited for her to do it again.

Other than the brief surprise, William couldn't read her reaction. Normally, he loved that she was reserved and even-tempered. He didn't want to worry about her flying off the handle. But once in a while, he wanted to see some clear emotion. Was she open to this subject or annoyed with him for bringing it up?

"That's probably not the impression you were trying to give." William spoke slowly, waiting for a signal to press ahead or shut up. "I just want you to know that I understand the... This is good for me, too. I get meals and company and I don't want you to move out, but obviously marriage would mean, uh, changes."

"Yeah, I wasn't really trying to suggest anything," Kay said.

She sounded extremely nervous, but there was good nervous and there was bad nervous. She said she wasn't trying to suggest it. That wasn't the same as saying it was a terrible idea.

"I know," he said. He wasn't sure he did.

"I just had a lot of thoughts in my head and some spilled out."

"Is it okay if we talk about it?"

She shrugged at him. Shrugged!

William was convinced she used the gesture to put on a brave front, not because she was actually indifferent. It only bugged him that she was so good at appearing relaxed because he was still trying to figure out if she was good nervous or bad nervous. Was she secretly hoping he was going to suggest what she hadn't meant to suggest? Or was she afraid he was leading up to an idea she'd have to reject?

For better or worse, he intended to pursue an answer. "What do you think about... you said you wished we were... Have you thought about it enough to think we could really make it work?"

Pete got tired of standing. Kay helped him down and watched him crawl towards a toy. Then she turned back, looked right into William's eyes for a change. "I can't stop thinking about it. Now. Like I said, I wasn't thinking ahead for a long time. I just wanted to get through each day because... because partly I was afraid to imagine my life without Beth. And partly I was so overwhelmed by the babies I didn't have time to... Anyway, I'm ready to make plans. And I can't help but keep coming back to the fact that everything would be easier if..." She bit her lip and the end of the sentence as she dropped her eyes to the carpet. She looked up again only enough to smile at Will across the table as she pushed his runaway truck back towards him.

William finished the sentence for her in his head. If things were different between us. Could they make things different? Because all he needed was permission. "We do get along almost like a couple. We want... I think we're picturing very similar futures. Except, um..." Suddenly he wondered if they were talking about the same thing. Maybe she meant that life would be easier if they could get married without actually changing the relationship. His eyes moved unconsciously to his bedroom door. Or at least it was unconscious until he did it. Then the door seemed like the most prominent thing in the room.

Kay noticed, though she continued to pretend she wasn't looking at him at all.

William felt heat creeping up the back of his neck. He was in way too deep to try to wade out now though. "So you thought about... and it wasn't... it, uh..." Okay. Perhaps he'd gotten in deep enough to start drowning. He reached out for a different way to approach the topic. "When you were thinking of an ideal future and being married with children, were you thinking of *more* children?"

"That was... well, it was another thing that made me... if I did have more kids I'd like them to actually grow up with Will and Pete and if I end up with a ten-year gap they might not really feel like siblings."

"So you were planning on trying for more kids in this ideal future and... and there was nothing in the picture that made you think it wouldn't work with me? You know, practically speaking."

Kay shook her head slowly, which was encouraging. She also looked as though she was trying not to smile, which seemed to be a point in favor of good nervous.

William realized he was starting to smile as well. He had to guess what that meant, too. Regardless, some of the heat in the room dissipated. "I'm imagining myself at the center of a big pro/con list in your head. And the pro list is sort of winning."

"Something like that."

"The pros aren't all negatives, are they?"

Kay laughed outright and finally seemed to relax. "That's not what pro means."

"Does the pro side have anything that doesn't start with I wouldn't? Like I wouldn't have to quit a good job, I wouldn't have to endure first dates, I wouldn't have to borrow that annoying guy's truck again." He flashed a smile as he reminded her of her words.

"You didn't tell him I said that, did you? He wasn't really *that* annoying anyway."

"Of course I didn't tell him."

"I think that would be on your list."

It would be on his list if he needed one. While Chris had refused even gas money for helping, he'd tried to be paid in probing questions. William had already decided to find someone else with a truck – or rent one – if he had to help Kay move out. It was actually sounding as though it wouldn't be necessary. "And you've thought about... you know that Will and Pete would eventually move out and then you'd be stuck with me."

"I'm not sure that would be *so* bad," she joked. "But seriously, do you think we'd suddenly stop being friends?"

"It happens to some couples."

Kay winced. "I suppose it does."

"I once heard my parents tell Annie and Jake to make sure they did something together that has nothing to do with the kids now and then," William said. "I don't know if that's like the key or just something that has worked for them, but it's, uh... something."

"Worth a try," Kay said.

Pete had crawled back and was climbing onto her lap. She fell backwards to let him pretend to tackle her. Will practically threw his car in his rush to put it down to join the pile. William sensed he was about to lose the momentum of the conversation. He had to get in one more question to be sure she was thinking about being married the same way he was. "And if we had other kids..." A deliberate pause to let that implication sink in. "They'd also eventually leave us."

Kay was laughing and trying to sit up so the boys could knock her down again. Perhaps William hadn't paused long enough. She glanced at him though, enough to indicate that she'd heard. She managed to sit up with a little boy wrapped in each arm. They were pushing on her shoulders to get her to fall again. Before she let them win, she said, "You went to the cemetery with me at Christmas."

Her comment at first seemed to be an attempt to change the subject. Then William wondered if she was trying to say that they already shared some types of intimacy. "And you think that would make it okay for…"

There was a sigh mixed in with her laugh. She didn't turn away from Will and Pete as they climbed on her, but she was clearly speaking to William when she said, "You're such a guy. You have a one-track mind, don't you?"

"Right now, yes. Because it feels like we're going in circles around that track, and I only want to know that you're sure that…"

A timer was beeping in the kitchen. Kay stood up and handed Pete to William, who also took hold of Will's hand to keep the boys out of the kitchen while she had the oven open. Kay pulled the pizza out and began to set the table while it cooled. William buckled Pete into his high chair wondering if he was going to need to finish the uncomfortable question to get an answer. He wanted to know, but he didn't want to ask because the answer might be no.

Kay began to cut up a slice for Will. "Let's just say," she said, keeping her eyes on the pizza, "that I know what marriage is. And I want the real thing."

16

$\mathcal{K}$ay was looking forward to dinner with Annie and Jake more than any week since she'd been tricked into agreeing to every week. She desperately needed to talk to someone. William was always her first choice, but since she needed to talk *about* William, he was out.

Kay had grown to consider Annie a friend. She wasn't sure they were close enough for a private, very personal discussion, but she just could not believe what William had done. She had to talk to someone. She couldn't talk to him. It would have to be Annie.

There was no chance for a private talk around the crowded dinner table. Afterwards, Kay alternated between hoping an opportunity would present itself and hoping one would not. Annie took Pete into the quiet room to look at pictures in board books.

Kay was watching from the doorway. Everyone else was still in the living room. William could step into the kitchen at any moment though. He'd probably hear her if she stayed in the doorway. If she went farther into the room though, she wouldn't see him coming.

It might have been the Holy Spirit whispering to Jake, and it might have been the nice weather. For whatever reason, he announced that he was taking the girls outside for kickball and invited William to join them. The three girls ran through the kitchen and out the back door with Jake right behind them. William was carrying Will.

"Do you want me to take him?" Kay asked.

"Oh, no," William said. "Will's gonna play, too."

"You think he can kick a ball?"

"I'm not sure, but he can definitely chase it and pick it up." He bounced Will in his arms. "Come on, buddy, we're going to work on your fielding skills."

"Excellent," Jake said. "You want in, Kay? You can be on my team."

"No, thanks. I'll stay inside." Kay hadn't decided if she had the courage to talk about what William did, but she was going to take the chance to try. She moved into the quiet room and sat in a beanbag.

Annie was on the floor pointing out red things in a book about colors. She glanced up and gave a welcoming smile.

Kay couldn't say it, not suddenly. She was going to try to ease her way to serious through some gentler talk. "I like this quiet room idea."

Annie nodded appreciatively. "It would have been a pretty small dining room. This seemed like a better use for a family that doesn't really do formal. Tomato." She was talking to Pete at the same time.

"You and William seem to talk in here a lot."

"Fishy." They'd moved on to the orange page. "I guess he does end up in here sometimes."

"You guys seem really tight."

Annie nodded. "Block. The block is orange, too."

"It's kind of interesting how some siblings... Beth and I were best friends, but Sherry – my dad's wife – has a sister two years older just like Beth and they aren't... As far as I know there hasn't been a falling out or anything, they just sort of treat each other like cordial acquaintances. Then you and William are farther apart in age and not both girls, yet..."

"Banana." Annie's demeanor said she was paying more attention to Kay than the board book so it didn't feel at all rude that she was doing two things at once. "I think we're close because of Michael," she said. "This one's a ball. A yellow ball. William was three when Michael was born, and I was almost ten. All of a sudden, our parents had a lot going on with doctor visits and just figuring things out."

Pete closed the book and crawled towards the bookshelf for another one. Annie shifted her legs to face Kay straight on. "I don't want to make it sound like we turned to each other because our parents ignored us. That wasn't the case at all. I think they did a great job, uh, spreading the love around. It's just that I saw they were busy and wanted to help. I didn't know anything about taking care of a baby, especially one with special needs, so I took it upon myself to be in charge of William. I think there were plenty of times he resented having a big sister trying to mother him. But kids can't help enjoying being the center of someone's attention. I think the age and gender difference actually helped because it eliminated, or at least reduced, any sense of competition between us."

The observations made Annie sound very wise, like someone who could offer advice. Kay wasn't sure how much longer she could keep it inside anyway.

Pete had pulled another book from the shelf. He was flipping the pages too fast for Annie to point anything out, and she didn't try to slow him down.

"He called a priest," Kay blurted.

Annie's eyes widened. "William did?"

"He called a priest," Kay said again, "to talk about a wedding date."

"You guys are engaged?" Annie broke into a huge grin. "Congrat—"

Kay shook her head fast before Annie could get the word out.

The grin fell right off her face. "You're not?"

"I don't think so."

"You don't... *think* so?" Her eyebrows went up in a way that made Kay feel stupid.

"I don't know. We were talking about getting married."

"You talked about it," Annie said. "Did he ask you to marry him?"

"No. Not really. We were... we talked about it, but I thought it was only mostly hypothetical. And then a few days later he drops this bomb like oh by the way we have an appointment with Father David on Thursday to talk about scheduling a wedding and I'm... I didn't say anything. I didn't know what to say."

Annie clearly didn't know what to say either. She stared at Kay for a minute, then looked past her towards the back door. Finally, she asked, "Do you *want* to marry him?"

Yes. Kay did want to marry William, for all the practical reasons they talked about and for reasons she kept knitted into her soul. But she couldn't say yes, not when Annie and everyone else thought they were only friends. William thought they were only friends. She'd have to be pretty brave to admit she wanted to marry him. "I don't think he wants to marry me," she said to dodge.

"What makes you say that?" Annie asked. "He's the one who called Father David."

"Yeah, but... I'm afraid he just feels sorry for me or something. He's not..." She paused to subdue the blush, but it only gave her face more time to deepen the red. "He's not attracted to me."

"Oh, uh..." Annie looked confused for a moment before that emotion shifted to complete irritation. "He did not actually say that, did he?" Her muscles twitched as though she was preparing to run outside and smack William if he'd dared to utter such an unfortunate truth.

"Well, no, but… we've been friends," she emphasized the word, "for quite a while and that was his idea in the first place. Why would he abandon any dating plans if… you know?"

"I see." Annie sort of relaxed. Her mouth bunched up in an expression Kay couldn't read because it looked like guilt and guilt didn't make any sense. "Where, um, where do you think you two go from here?"

Kay gave the most exaggerated shrug she could manage. "I don't know. I just know that if we're not getting married, we need to establish that *not* in front of Father David. I see him at work. I…" She finished with a groan. Words had not been invented to describe the humiliation she feared.

Annie chuckled softly, but with sympathy. It felt as though she would be on Kay's side, if it was a situation that had sides. It didn't have sides though, only a swirl of how did this happen and what do I do about it. "All right." Annie straightened her face and her posture. "I noticed that you said if."

"What do you mean?"

"You said, '*if* we're not going to get married.' That leads me back to the question of… Do you want to marry William?"

Blood pounded in Kay's ears as her heart sped up. She didn't want to lie any more than she wanted to tell the truth, and that didn't leave a lot of options.

"You don't have to tell me," Annie said. "But you need to tell yourself. Because if you don't want to marry him, you'll have to tell him he misunderstood something. Before you sit down with a priest."

Kay clamped her teeth against the imaginary bullet. "He didn't misunderstand."

"Oh!" Annie smiled and tapped her finger against her lips to signal that the truth was safe with her. "Now we're getting somewhere," she said. "And I'm getting very curious. I think I would've liked to have been a fly on the wall during this conversation where you apparently talked about getting married without getting engaged and agreed to get married without actually agreeing to anything."

"Maybe I did." Kay wished she could go back and witness the conversation for herself. "But I… I thought I was agreeing in theory."

"In theory? How did this subject even come up to make you think it was hypothetical?"

"It was my fault." Kay started at the beginning and went through the messy conversations as fast as she could. She explained how she didn't want to quit her job or move out or look for a husband. She admitted that she'd accidentally wished out loud that she and William were married so she could stay comfortable. He'd caught her off guard when he brought it up again. Living on her own and separating the boys from William would be difficult. She couldn't help being honest about the fact that marrying him would solve a lot of her problems. "But he was so casual about everything. I thought he was saying what do you think about this, not do you think we should do this."

"And then he called a priest." Annie was sitting on the carpet and not a seat, but she was definitely on the edge of something. "He must have been less casual than he was letting on. You know how guys love to talk about their feelings."

Kay shook her head sadly. "I think the only feeling he has is entrapment. I made him feel responsible for… everything. I didn't mean to. Now he thinks he needs to rescue me again. I don't want to be a burden. He'll resent me eventually if we go through with a wedding."

The back door flew open as Bailey jumped into the house. "We won!" she shouted.

The others began to file in behind her.

Kay picked up Pete. If kickball was over, she couldn't talk to Annie anymore and might as well get the boys home to bed. She turned as William came inside. "How was the game? Did Will like it?"

"I think he had fun."

Jake came in right behind William. "Someone needs to work on those fielding skills," he said, "and it isn't Will."

"I missed an easy catch," William said. "But in my defense, I did not step on Taylor, which I think I would have done if I'd gotten to the ball."

"She didn't blame you for her mistakes." Jake was having fun with the taunting.

William only said, "Next week." Then he asked Kay if she was ready to leave.

They gathered everything they'd had when they arrived and said goodbyes. Kay was heading out the door first when Annie called her back.

"Oh, Kay? I found that sock Will lost last week. Hang on." She dashed around a corner to get it.

William went ahead to get Will strapped into his car seat. When Annie returned with the tiny sock, she got close and whispered, "Ask him."

Jake was herding the girls towards the stairs to get ready for bed.

"Ask him what?" Kay said.

"If you think you owe William anything, you owe it to him not to make assumptions about his motives. Make him tell you how he really feels."

Kay nodded. She had a feeling the sock was a lot easier to take than the advice.

17

Their appointment was at 6 PM. They needed to eat quickly to get to the church on time. William was in a hurry to get there anyway. Kay had hinted that she wanted to talk about something before the meeting. He guessed that she wondered how they should tell the priest that she'd agreed to marry a man she wasn't in love with.

William intended to take full responsibility for that. But it wasn't something he wanted to talk about more than once. He knew Kay was in a vulnerable position, and that she didn't feel the same about him as he did about her. None of that changed the fact that she needed him. Wasn't marriage, after all, a sacrament of service? He would vow to spend the rest of his life helping her and trying to give her whatever she needed. That sounded honorable.

On the other hand, he knew he wanted to marry her so badly he could probably justify any reason. William needed an outsider's opinion. He didn't know Father David outside of Sundays, but he didn't strike him as the kind of man to pull any punches. If it sounded to him as though William was taking advantage of Kay, he'd put a stop to any wedding plans.

Kay didn't say a word as she drove to the church. William sensed it was bad nervous keeping her quiet. He hoped it was the idea of a personal chat with someone she didn't know well and not the subject matter that was bothering her. What if she had changed her mind?

She pulled into a parking space at the back of the building, near the offices.

"This is where you park when you're coming to work?" he asked.

She nodded and shut off the car.

William unbuckled his seat belt. He reached for the door handle.

"Wait," Kay said. "Are you sure about this?"

"Yes." He answered quickly, then kicked himself. If she was trying to back out, he didn't need to pressure her.

"Just… before we go in, tell me I didn't talk you into this idea."

"I kind of thought I talked *you* into it."

Kay stared at him without smiling. "I'm serious," she said.

"So am I."

Pete was the most serious. He was screaming to be let out of his car seat immediately.

"You're not…" Kay glanced at the back seat, trying to hurry her thoughts. "You feel like you have good enough reasons to marry me?"

"Aren't we here to talk about all this with Father David?" William wasn't trying to be dismissive. It sounded dismissive after the words were out of his mouth though. He only wanted to point out that an objective mediator might be helpful.

Kay apparently agreed or gave up because she opened her door and jumped out to get Pete.

William also got out the front and turned to the back seat. He'd suggested they ask Annie and Jake to babysit, but Kay wanted to bring the boys. She said Father David should see how they worked as a family. William thought she might also be afraid Annie would ask why they needed a babysitter. It wasn't something he wanted to discuss with his sister yet. Pete and Will got to come.

The office was closed so they had to ring a doorbell and wait to be buzzed in. Kay went in first as the door clicked open. She stopped two steps over the threshold to let William move ahead of her. Father David was standing behind a large desk.

"Pleasure to see you, Kay," he said, stepping around the desk to offer a handshake. "And you must be William."

William took the offered hand and tried to respond with a firm, confident grip. He wasn't going to start with doubts. He was doing the right thing.

"Follow me back to my office," Father David said with a wave of his hand. "Let's get comfortable and then we'll get started."

There was a short hallway lined with religious artwork. Each picture had a small card in the corner with the name of the person or family who had donated it. Father David's office was at the end of the hallway and was obviously the largest room.

William knew from Kay that it doubled as the church's library. He might have guessed that since two of the walls were lined with bookshelves around five feet high. More decorative gifts hung above the shelves. A desk with a computer, a phone, and lots of papers and books was on one side of the room. A round table surrounded by four chairs sat on the other side.

Father David gestured to the table. "Have a seat."

He closed the door before he pulled out the chair on the other side of Kay for himself.

The room had flat carpet and the chairs had wheels. Kay quietly rolled her chair closer to William. She appeared to be settling Pete on her lap. William noticed the deliberate direction and the subtle movement made him feel good, protective.

"I think he's gotten bigger." Father David was looking at Pete. It had been at least two months since Kay took him to work. The baby probably had grown.

"Heavier, too," Kay said.

"So…" The priest leaned back in his chair as his eyes moved back and forth, taking in the picture in front of him. "The two of you are looking to get married."

William got the impression that Father David was already appraising their worthiness for such an event. It made him glad the priest already knew Will and Pete's backstory so he didn't have to explain why he showed up to talk about getting married with two babies in tow.

"Why don't we start with easy questions? Where did you meet?"

"At work," Kay said.

"We used to work for the same company."

"And how long ago did you meet?"

They answered together, but Kay said, "Two years," and William said, "Three years."

She glanced nervously at William as though they were about to be caught in a lie.

"I guess it hasn't been quite three years," he said, "maybe closer to two and a half."

Kay nodded meekly.

Father David smiled. He looked around sixty. His gray hair was sprinkled with darker patches and his eyes with lines. He was of course wearing all black with a white collar. There was a weird crease across the front of his shirt and one of the buttons was on the verge of falling off. The imperfections made him less intimidating. The smile helped, too. "I'm not going to bite," he said.

Kay didn't look entirely convinced. She was putting more effort and concentration into entertaining Pete than necessary. And she was sending furtive glances to William, asking him to do the talking.

There wasn't much point in waiting to come clean about their situation. William planned to take the heat if there was going to be any heat. "Well, Father, we should go ahead and be honest with you."

He kept smiling, but he nodded his agreement that honesty was the only option.

William opened his mouth and realized he didn't know how to word the truth. He couldn't say he wasn't in love with Kay. Saying she wasn't in love with him might be true, but it'd put her on the spot. It almost sounded like an accusation. They were in this together so he needed to say something that began with we. "We, um, haven't exactly been dating. We didn't arrive at this decision the way most people do."

Father David put both his arms on the table and leaned forward. He made a silly face at Will before he went back to scrutinizing the adults. "What exactly are you trying to tell me?"

"We're friends," Kay said. To William it sounded like a plea to stop looking at her.

"Good friends," he added, trying to draw some attention.

Father David may have heard the plea. He kept his forearms on the table but sat back a little and focused on William. "You want to be a dad to these boys."

William nodded, though it sounded more like an observation than a question.

"Dads are important." The priest took a big breath and sat straighter. He appeared to be preparing for a speech or a sermon, and William hoped it wasn't about to turn into a lecture. "I think the two of you want me to believe you are not in love when you actually mean you are not infatuated. Infatuation is a feeling, the feeling that makes people make goo-goo eyes at each other. Love is an action, a choice. It's the conscious decision to treat another person with respect and kindness and I see love in this room so I'm not going to tell you that you can't get married if that's what you're worried about. Infatuation, in most cases, fades if it doesn't disappear completely. A marriage based on a true friendship probably has a better chance of being happy than one built on infatuation *provided…*" He held up his hand between William and Kay as he emphasized the word to make sure he had their full attention. "You both understand this is a lifelong commitment and not an until this little guy goes off to college commitment."

William nodded.

Kay nodded.

Father David continued, pausing occasionally to check for more nodding. "You understand that your primary job is to help each other grow in holiness, not to satisfy earthly whims. You will remember to keep God at the center of your union. And you will welcome any other children he sees fit to give you."

Even Will was nodding. He twisted his neck to look up at William and copied him.

"All right then." Father David slid his chair to the desk behind him and reached for a small spiral-bound book. He moved back and slapped the day planner open on the table. He began to flip through the pages as he said, "Let's talk dates. If you want to do the ceremony with a full mass, it'll have to be a Saturday and we're booked pretty far out. If you'd rather keep it simple, we can do a short ceremony after one of the daily masses. I prefer to do those on Fridays, but I'm not married to the day." He smiled at his own joke, then looked up for some input.

Kay looked at William for input, too.

He said, "I think we'd rather go with simple."

The question didn't leave her eyes.

Was he wrong to assume that just because she was okay with

a practical marriage that she didn't want a fancy wedding? "Unless you want..." He turned to Father David. "I'm sorry. We didn't really talk about, well, the wedding itself."

"Don't apologize for that," Father David said with a laugh. "I wish everyone came to me having talked more about the marriage than the wedding. Go on and discuss it." He shoved his planner to the side as though he had all the time in the world.

"What do you want?" Kay asked. Her voice was soft, as though she hoped only William would hear her question.

He could hardly believe this wonderful woman was sitting there planning to marry him. It would be selfish to want anything else. "I'm happy with whatever makes you happy," he said.

Kay bit back a smile with a slight eye roll. She apparently thought he was giving her some sort of line. "Do you want to invite people?"

"Just family." William remembered Bailey and Ariana had recently had her playing wedding with their dolls. "Annie's girls would love it if we let them hold some flowers, but it wouldn't have to be an official role or anything."

"You, um... if we get married on a Friday, you'd have to take the day off work. Or at least half a day." She was looking at him doubtfully, like using up a vacation day might be a deal breaker.

William's gut clenched with worry. Either Kay wanted to give him a reason to back out or she was working up to admitting she wanted out. Unless she just wanted a reason to go for the more elaborate Saturday wedding? He latched onto that hope. "Do you want to get married on a Saturday?"

Her head moved side to side an inch or so before she turned Pete around and sat him on the table to look at him. She gave him an everything's okay smile that probably even the baby didn't fall for.

"Kay, just tell me what you're thinking. Have you changed your mind about this?" William glanced at the priest, who seemed happy to let them talk but didn't appear to have any intention of letting them do it in private.

Kay's eyes shifted to Father David and back, too. She took a breath. Then she tried another one. "It's just that… I'm worried… that I trapped you into this."

"What are you talking about?"

"I'm worried that…" Her voice got quieter. "I feel like I've been begging you for help for so long that maybe you think you don't have a choice anymore."

"Have you not been paying attention?" William thought his motives had been transparent from the start. He figured she didn't want to see it. He was going to clear up a few things to get rid of her guilt even if it meant showing her the truth. "Yes. You called me the day of the accident and asked me to bring you car seats. Did you even ask me to drive you to the hospital? No. Did you call for help on the next day or the day after that or the day after that? No. I offered to help. Did you ask if you could move in with me? No. I offered. Just like I am offering to marry you. I want to help you, and I want to marry you. If you want something else you better say so before I get Father David to put us down for the next available Friday. *In ink*." He tried to end on a light note because it was starting to feel as though he was yelling at Kay, which was not the best way to point out how much he cared about her.

Father David began to flip the pages again. He sent William a quick wink. It appeared he approved of the little speech.

The only one who said anything was Pete. And he didn't say any clear words, just babbling noises while he tried to grab Kay's face. She seemed to relax though, and after a minute she said, "A simple Friday ceremony sounds good."

"July 21ˢᵗ?" The priest tapped the open page and looked up.

"That's Will's birthday," Kay said. Her eyes bugged out a little. William guessed it had more to do with the date being less than three months away than it being anyone's birthday.

William had expected to wait longer as well. Perhaps they would have if they'd wanted a big, fancy wedding. This was better. "That will be great."

"All right." Father David made a note. "Mrs. Adams will help Kay get the paperwork in order and Deacon Mike does the premarital counseling. You'll need to schedule at least two sessions with him between now and... let's say the beginning of July. Don't wait until the week of in case it needs to be rescheduled for any reason. Do you have any questions for me?"

Kay shook her head and glanced at the diaper bag at her feet. It was clear she was getting ready to pick it up and leave.

"No," William said. "Is there anything else you need from us?"

"I've seen enough." He pushed his chair back from the table to stand. Then he thanked them for coming as he opened the office door.

William also thanked the priest for his time. He sort of wondered what the man had seen. There was something like amusement in his tone. William shrugged it off though, grateful that he'd gotten permission to marry Kay, in addition to a day for it to happen.

She led the way outside again. "The boys were so good in there," she said on the way to the car.

"I know." It was something else for which William could be grateful. "I thought for sure Will was going to want down to start pulling books off the shelves."

"He had lots of books," Will said.

205

"Too late, buddy. You missed your chance."

"Can I read them?"

"I don't think he had any books you'd want to read. Didn't look like ones with pictures."

"I want to walk." Will was already fighting to be put down, book opportunity a distant memory.

"Okay. Hold my hand." William set him on the sidewalk and grabbed the tiny hand. There were only four cars in the whole parking lot, but it was a habit and likely a good one. He opened the back door and let Will climb in on his own before he buckled the straps.

Kay had buckled Pete faster and was already behind the wheel. When William got in, she didn't start the car right away. She turned to him with an expression that looked... happy. "Does this... does this mean we're officially engaged now?"

That was a thought that made William pretty happy, too. "Yes. I guess we have an announcement to make."

18

$\mathcal{K}$ay had been so worried when they went to see Father David. She'd painted a dire picture with her expectations. She was sure he was going to accuse her of taking advantage of William. Instead, he made it sound as though they'd arrived at a healthy decision. And William did not feel taken advantage of.

He'd been so clear about that. Kay walked out of that meeting with her spirits soaring because William said straight out that he wanted to marry her. The way he said it made her believe he wanted to marry her for her, not only because of his love for Pete and Will or because of any sense of obligation. She'd felt truly engaged to a man she loved.

Doubts began to creep back as their relationship returned to normal.

Normal was good. They talked about wedding plans without awkwardness. They disagreed without arguing. They went to their first session with the deacon and actually enjoyed it.

The man began the session by saying that no marriage could survive as a fifty-fifty partnership. If both spouses believed they only needed to give fifty percent, that would lead to keeping score, watching the balance, and bitter feelings. He talked briefly about many topics, including conflict resolution and budget planning. Every topic ended with a reminder about both spouses needing to give one hundred percent to the relationship and each task within it.

William and Kay heard so many reminders that they began to tease each other about it. Once Kay had William browning a pan of ground beef for dinner. When he accidentally spilled some over the side of the pan, Kay didn't roll her eyes at the mess or get annoyed. She accused him of not giving one hundred percent to the task. When she admitted a load of laundry had been sitting in the washer for hours, he accused her of the same. They both laughed.

Normal was good. But normal didn't look like two people who were engaged. Normal looked like two people who were friends. William never put his arm around her or touched her hand. He never kissed her. Kay began to worry that it would be too uncomfortable to make the shift after the wedding.

Then she'd tell herself she was nuts. He was male, after all. Surely he wouldn't be satisfied to be married without enjoying all the benefits of being married. He was the one who tried to drive that point home when they discussed the possibility.

But the worries always came back. William would sit next to her to watch TV and seem completely unaware that she was close. What if they'd been friends so long he couldn't see her any differently than he saw his sister? If he had some mental block against physical contact, that could be difficult to overcome. It was something that should be addressed before they stood in front of Father David on the 21st.

Kay had already flipped the calendar. The date was staring at her in the kitchen. Only the word wedding was written in that square. The one word didn't seem to adequately describe the life-changing event that would take place. And yet, Kay reflected, her source of worry was that her name was the only thing that would change.

"I want milk. I want milk." Will was behind her tugging fruitlessly on the handle of the refrigerator.

She smiled at him to show he had her attention. "Do you want me to get out your sippy cup?"

He nodded and tugged harder. "I want milk."

"Can you ask nicely?"

"Milk, please."

She opened the fridge and passed him the cup of milk. He threw his head back for a drink. Pete crawled into the kitchen, sat up and threw his arms in the air in a fuss.

"You want milk, too?"

He seemed happy that she had interpreted correctly. Kay handed him a sippy cup, and he did a very good imitation of his brother. Pete was beginning to understand a lot. He'd likely start talking soon. And walking sooner. It might almost be time to stop thinking of them as babies. That was a scary thought.

The door to the garage opened before she got too caught up in the quick passage of time. William said, "Hi," as he walked in.

Will grinned. "Daddy!" His word was more of an announcement than a greeting.

William looked pleased by it either way. He planned to adopt the boys after he married Kay. Kay had taken to referring to him as Daddy in front of the little ones. Will had gotten used to calling him William so she expected it might take him a while to adjust. She had no intention to correct him if he stuck with William. But Will changed to using Daddy without batting an eye. He adjusted faster than Kay did.

"How was work, Daddy?" She winced at the odd inflection in the word.

William put the mail he'd picked up on the way in on the counter. "I'm not sure you're giving one hundred percent to that new name."

She wrinkled her nose defiantly at him.

"It was your idea." William glanced around the kitchen. "Am I helping with dinner tonight?"

"Do you want to help with dinner?"

"I never want to help with dinner." He leaned over as he spoke and snagged Pete into a hug. He picked up both boys frequently and patted their heads and generally seemed comfortable showering Pete and Will with physical affection. Kay noticed this. And she couldn't remember the last time William had touched her when he wasn't handing her a child.

She dismissed those thoughts for later. "Since you're so excited about helping me..." She waited for his reaction and was rewarded with a playful glare. "I thought you could make a salad. No cooking. Just chopping and mixing."

"Ah, salad. I've done that before. I'm practically a salad expert. Right, Pete?"

Pete smiled and handed William the cup he'd finished by smacking him in the chest with it.

William put Pete on the floor, the cup in the fridge, then his hands in the sink for washing. He was not a salad expert. His lettuce pieces were way too big to be considered bite-sized. He held the tomatoes so tightly when he sliced them that he squeezed out all the juice, and he had to take a break when he somehow managed to flick a tidbit of onion into his own eye. Then he tossed half the salad onto the counter when he tried to mix it.

Will laughed at the salad mess as though it had been done purely for his amusement. His adorable giggles probably helped Kay keep her temper in check. She no longer thought William simply refused to learn how to cook because he did seem to be trying. She figured it was a confidence issue. He might not be competent in the kitchen until he believed he could be competent. Or until he had a lot more practice. But she knew what she'd signed up for.

After dinner, he helped her get Will and Pete ready for bed. She didn't have to give directions for every little thing at that time of day. They worked as a team. Kay had separated the cribs after the boys figured out they could grab each other through the bars.

William stood with Pete in front of his crib and Kay stood with Will on the other side of the room. The two adults sang the Our Father together while Will threw in a word here and there.

The warm bass notes and intermittent sweetness completed the prayer in a way Kay could not have imagined those first few nights when she was just trying to cope. Even Pete made a cute humming noise with the amen. They sounded like a family and even that off-key line was beautiful.

Kay and William left the room through separate doors, William towards the living room and Kay into the bathroom for a shower. When Kay was ready for bed, she joined William. She usually found him sitting in front of the TV, usually flipping rather aimlessly through the channels. This time he was sitting at the table with a deck of cards. They were split into piles, and he appeared to be playing War by himself.

"Are you playing War by yourself?" Kay asked.

He gave a combined nod and shrug. "I was bored."

"You still look bored."

"I am." He looked up from the riveting six and ten battle. "Want to play something with me?"

"All right." She pulled out the chair across from him.

"War?"

"No."

He smashed all his piles together. "How about Spike and Alice?"

"Sure."

William grabbed a second deck and began to shuffle all the

cards together. The game was actually called Spite and Malice. William had inadvertently renamed it as a kid. The story was that after Annie taught him the game, he'd told his parents they'd been playing Spike and Alice. The family got a laugh, then called it the new name from then on because it sounded a whole lot nicer.

Kay won the game mostly due to luck because she was very distracted. Early on, she'd accidentally kicked William's shin under the table. Her feet were bare so she knew it hadn't hurt him. He'd moved out of the way, and she couldn't help but wonder what would have happened if it hadn't been an accident.

Would he have pulled his leg back if she put her foot on it on purpose? Was he just trying to give her some room or avoiding the touch? They were getting married in less than three weeks. She needed to know. But with his legs under his chair she couldn't find out. Not without sliding herself down in her chair and that was just weird.

William put the cards away in a drawer in the kitchen. It was already around the time Kay normally went to bed. She stood in the middle of the living room trying to figure out what to do when he returned. She needed to know how he'd respond to a deliberate touch, but she didn't know where to start. Take his hand? Just stand in the middle of the room holding hands? Weird.

Could she kiss him? Just out of the blue act as though a good night kiss was a regular thing? The thought sent adrenaline coursing through her body. Unfortunately, it wasn't the good kind of adrenaline. It was more like a fight or flight response.

Maybe a hug. She'd hugged him before. Mostly right after Beth died. She could do that. But hugs could be platonic. All the other hugs had been platonic. It wouldn't necessarily answer the question she desperately wanted to answer. And maybe she was just making it hard because she was so scared. There was only one answer she wanted.

She stood frozen in indecision long enough that William noticed. "Are you waiting for something?" he asked.

"You," she said.

"Oh?" He sounded either intrigued or worried but mostly like he wasn't sure if he should be intrigued or worried. He moved so that he was standing about two feet in front of her and said, "Me what?"

"I wanted to ask you something."

"Okay."

"Are you, um…" She thought she was smiling because he sounded nervous, but maybe it was her own nerves shaking the smile loose because nothing was funny. There was nothing funny about having to ask her fiancé if he was worried about the honeymoon. Nor was it funny that her mouth refused to say those words in any order.

William flashed an encouraging smile.

Maybe she could come at the question from a different angle. "It's just that, with Will and Pete, you don't seem to have any trouble, you know, showing physical affection right now."

"You're not really worried that would change if we have more kids, are you? I'm sure I wouldn't treat them any differently if I had biological children." He looked a lot more serious.

"Oh, no! No, I didn't even think of that."

"Then just tell me what you're talking about."

"Okay." She steeled her nerves. She was just going to ask. "Why don't you ever… you don't act that way around me. Is it my imagination that you avoid touching me?"

His eyes darted to the ground for a moment. There was enough guilt to admit it wasn't her imagination. "I didn't think… You're not a touchy-feely person. I remember my mom tried to hug you when I introduced you two and… Well, from the look on your face someone might have thought she was coming at you with a chloroform rag."

Kay felt her eyes give away some guilt as well. She hadn't realized she was so obvious about avoiding hugs.

"I've always tried to respect your... preference. You want me to start carrying you around on my shoulders now?" There was an almost petulant tone to his question, as though he thought it was unfair of her to change the rules.

The rules were about to change though. If William couldn't get on board with that... "Of course not," Kay said. "Of course I'm not suggesting you should start treating me like one of the kids. But just because I prefer that strangers keep their hands off me... And yes, anyone I've just met counts as a stranger..." She tried not to let defensiveness sidetrack the conversation. But chloroform? Really? "That doesn't mean I'd feel the same about someone, uh, about someone I was about to marry. I'm just worried that since... What if there's no, uh, chemistry?"

"Oh." His voice wavered at the same time his feet brought him closer.

Kay was a little undone by what appeared to be a mixed reaction. That triggered some unfortunate babbling. "Between us, I mean," she said. "That would be a problem, right? We were talking about potential baby names last week. I shouldn't have to spell out how a lack of chemistry could be a problem. What if we got married and then... and we couldn't... or we needed... because it would be bad if it wasn't good. Right?"

William's hand came up between them while Kay was talking. She couldn't tell if he intended to gently touch her face or cover her mouth to shut her up. He put it back down without doing either. "We talked about this before we started making plans. I thought we agreed it wouldn't be a problem."

"Yeah, we talked about it, but…" He was close enough to kiss her. She tingled with awareness and desire. Yet dampening the mood was a feeling that she was practically begging him to pretty please try to kiss her. She wouldn't say exactly that, but even in her head the words made her feel pathetic. "We talked, but we didn't… we haven't… I think we need to test the waters."

"You need to test… *right now?*"

"We need to find out before we're married."

"Are you trying to say that unless… if this test doesn't…" He stumbled over the question.

If Kay thought she felt pathetic before, it was nothing compared to the realization that William was stalling. If he needed to psych himself up to kiss her then she absolutely didn't want him to try. She backed away, the adrenaline ignited stronger than before and she chose flight. "I'm sorry. This was a terrible idea. Good night."

19

*K*ay fed the boys and disappeared into her bedroom with them before William could say anything to her. It might have been for the best considering how much trouble he had stringing words together early in the morning. They needed to talk soon though. He'd thought she meant springing a chemistry test on him was a terrible idea. It wasn't until after she'd gone to bed that he wondered if she actually meant marrying him was a terrible idea.

It was Tuesday. He thought about canceling dinner with Annie and Jake to allow more time to talk to Kay. But if Annie didn't feed them then Kay would need to make dinner. It would be a bad idea to make that change without consulting Kay. Before he had a chance to ask her, she texted him that he should go straight to Annie's after work because she wasn't feeling well.

He was almost relieved to hear that. Maybe the disappearing act that morning didn't have anything to do with her being angry or uncomfortable around him. Maybe she was sick. On the other hand, he hated to think of her being sick and trying to take care of two babies. He went home after work to check on Kay. He figured the least he could do was take Will and Pete off her hands for an hour or two.

Kay looked surprised when he walked through the door even though he generally came home from work around the same time, he had told her he was coming, and it was his house. "I thought you were going straight to Annie's," she said.

"No, I wanted to check on you. Didn't you get my text?"

She shook her head and pushed a little car around on the table. Will had another car. His was chasing Kay's and ramming the back of it. "Gentle," she reminded him.

"How are you feeling?" William asked.

Kay turned her head away, but he was pretty sure she was trying to hide an exasperated look. "I'm fine. Aren't you hungry?"

"I thought you were sick."

"There are different kinds of not feeling well," she said. "I just want to be alone."

Her fairly polite words about wanting time alone sounded an awful lot like get lost. The situation was worse than William thought. Would she even let him close enough to try again? He decided to offer space first. "Do you want me to take the boys with me?"

"You don't have to do that."

"I'd like to."

She looked up at him for a moment with something very sad in her eyes before she nodded. "I'll get the bag ready for you."

Pete was sitting on the carpet dropping a bunch of little cars into an empty cereal box. William knelt next to him. "What are you doing with these cars?"

Pete answered the question by pouring the cars out with a big smile on his face.

"Do you want to go to Annie's with me?"

"I want to go! I want to go!" Will abandoned his car. He'd mostly lost interest when he no longer had Kay's to crash into.

"Find your shoes."

Will ran off and returned carrying his shoes a few moments later. He handed them to William then sat without being asked to make his feet accessible.

Kay handed him the diaper bag just as he got the second shoe secured. "Are you sure you don't want to come?"

She shook her head with her eyes on the cars Pete had dumped.

"Should I stay home, too, so we can talk?"

She did look at him and her eyes said no. "You got the boys excited now. Go let your sister feed you." She pulled her car keys from a bag on the counter and handed them to William.

He'd only taken the boys a few places without Kay, once to a park and one random trip to the store for batteries. It felt a little strange and a lot like a member of the family was missing.

He knew someone would ask where Kay was the second he got through the door. It was Annie who asked as she let him in. But then Jake asked as he came into the living room. Bailey and Ariana came downstairs five minutes later and asked about Kay, too. The third time William said she wasn't feeling well, it began to feel like a lie. Kay had said there were different kinds of not feeling well. That was the truth. It only felt like a lie when William said it because he felt as though he was covering his own inadequacies. He was the one who had caused her to be not feeling well.

There wasn't much time to dwell on her absence during dinner, even when it was the only thing he could think about. Will and Pete seemed to require more attention than when Kay was there, and she wasn't there to help. He cut up food on one side, then retrieved a fork from the floor on the other side, then refilled a cup, then cut some more food, then stopped a handful of food from hitting the floor, and so on.

Annie was smirking on and off. She reached out to assist a few times, but pulled back without actually helping. It seemed she enjoyed the show more than tending babies. Maybe she could restrain herself because she was expecting another one of her own in a few months.

As Jake cleared the table, the girls started asking to watch a movie.

"Isn't that the same one they watched last week?" William asked.

Annie sighed. "And almost every day since." It had been a birthday present for Taylor and apparently a successful one, depending on the interpretation. "I'll get it started."

William cleaned up Will, who wanted to watch, too, then got Pete out of the high chair. He set Pete in front of the movie, but he lost interest about the same time the three adults were ready to begin a board game. Pete sat on William's lap during the game, trying to grab the pieces. William had his hands full trying to do well in the game while keeping little pieces out of Pete's hands and especially out of his mouth. He was a little relieved when Jake's phone rang.

"It's my mom," he said. "Do you guys mind if we pause for a few minutes?" He was already stepping away from the table.

"Go ahead." William pushed his chair back and turned Pete around to sit on the edge of the table facing him. "You just can't wait until you're old enough to play this game, can you?"

The baby smiled as he stuck his fist in his mouth. There was nothing in that fist so it was fine. William looked over the little head to Annie on the other side of the table.

His sister had her hands clasped over her round belly and her eyes widened expectantly as soon as she met his gaze. She seemed to be suggesting he go ahead and spill his guts right now instead of making her go through the trouble of worming it out of him.

It wasn't going to happen. Not this time. There was no way he was going to admit how he'd chickened out. He still didn't fully understand what had happened. It was as though Kay had ambushed him and said, "You have one kiss to generate some serious chemistry or the wedding's off."

Who wouldn't cave under that kind of pressure? And who would tell his sister about it?

"The girls are very excited about their new dresses," Annie said. "I had a time convincing them they had to save them for the wedding."

William nodded but kept his guard up. She planned to talk until he was relaxed, then start asking questions.

"I told them they could wear the dresses every Sunday after the wedding if they want."

"I believe they'd do just that."

"Of course, I have to admit I liked having an excuse to buy my girls matching dresses, too. They're going to be so cute."

"We'll have to make sure we get lots of pictures," William said. *If there's a wedding.* He didn't add that part out loud though he couldn't help thinking it. He wished he knew why Kay suddenly needed proof. They'd talked and agreed that a physical relationship would be fine. They were, after all, human, with normal human sensations. As long as they could communicate, they could figure out how to make things work between them. And they would hopefully have many years to figure it out.

Kay had noticed that he deliberately kept his hands off her even after they were engaged and planning a wedding. He had to ask himself why he hadn't tried to test the waters, as she put it. The answer seemed to be that he was simply being patient, though that patience was certainly a struggle. He believed that sharing vows and the knowledge that they were joined in a sacred, lifelong union would cause Kay to feel differently and respond differently. He had to believe that.

Because the only other explanation was that he was subconsciously waiting until they were married so Kay couldn't back out. If he was doing that on any level, he probably deserved to have her back out.

"William?" Annie appeared to be waiting for something.

He must have missed a question. "What?"

She smiled, enjoying his distraction too much. "I asked if Kay had her dress yet. I thought she said she was hoping to find one this week."

"I don't know," he said. "I think I'm not supposed to see it, right? She might have gotten something without telling me."

"She could tell you without describing it or anything. She said she wanted something simple she could wear again."

"I really don't care what she wears," William said. "Only that she shows up."

"Wait." Annie's eyes got big. She leaned forward. "Do you think she might not show up?"

William shook his head. Despite the current trouble, he still believed Kay was going to marry him. "No, I didn't mean that. I just meant I'll be happy no matter what she has on."

"Huh." Annie tipped her head as though she wasn't sure she believed him. "Is that the real reason she's not here tonight?"

"There's no *real reason*." He sounded irritable, which to Annie probably sounded suspicious. "Are you going to make lasagna next week? I think it's been a long time."

Annie gave an amused sigh. Changing the subject likely sounded twice as suspicious. "I'm not sure that's a summer food."

"Lasagna cares what season it is?"

Jake returned to his chair and tried to pick up the conversation. "Why are we personifying lasagna?"

"I was just explaining that it's better on a cold day," Annie said.

"And I think we should have it next week." William tried to remember where he was in the game.

Jake appeared to be paying more attention to the game as well because he sounded distracted when he said he'd have to side with William. "I'd never turn down your lasagna."

Will got bored of the movie shortly before they finished the game. He sat on Annie's lap trying to grab her pieces. He was a little more successful than his brother but also more receptive to instructions. Annie showed him where to put the pieces for her.

By the time the game was over, William was ready to leave. Kay had her space and now he was going to have his say. And there weren't going to be a lot of words. He'd chickened out once, but he wasn't going to do it again. She wanted to marry him, he was sure of that because she had spelled out a lot of reasons. And if she wanted to marry him, it stood to reason that she wanted to feel some sparks. He might just have enough to send her way.

Kay was sitting on the couch with a book that she immediately shoved aside when he came in. She smiled at Will when he ran up to her and took his hand to find pajamas. They got the boys ready for bed quickly though it seemed to take longer than usual because of William's desire to get Kay alone. As they sang the Our Father, he thought to ask her to postpone her shower. If she went into the bathroom now, he probably wouldn't see her until morning.

He said good night to Pete and noticed a piece of paper on Kay's bed as he turned around. The sun set late enough in the summer that he could read it clearly with no lights in the room. It was a copy of her résumé. It included her current job.

She would only need that if she was looking for a new job and she'd only need a new job if she was planning on moving out and she'd only be planning on moving out if she wasn't going to go through with a wedding. It didn't take any breadcrumbs to follow that trail. And yet, William was lost.

"What's this?" He picked up the paper.

Kay shushed him before she whispered, "It's my résumé."

"I know what it is," he said, fully aware that he'd just asked what it was.

Will's head popped up at the commotion. Kay waved at William to leave the room with her so she could close the door. He followed her down the hall to somewhere between dazed and panicked. He must really not have had doubts for the paper to have given him such a shock. She wasn't even going to give him a chance?

Kay spoke first. "I didn't get a... Well, I did. I just couldn't work up the nerve to talk to Father David today. I'll try to tell him tomorrow."

"Tell him what, exactly?"

"You know what." Her voice was quiet and her expression bordering on miserable. She looked as though *he* was the one wounding *her*.

"But I don't know why." He wrapped his arms around her without thinking about anything besides the fact that he didn't want to let go. She couldn't leave him, not now when they were so close to having a life together.

In the middle of the desperation came the realization that Kay was holding on just as tightly. Her head was on his shoulder and her arms clasped around his back as though she didn't want to let go either. It felt wonderful, except for the part that didn't make any sense. That was the part that made him tear himself from the embrace just far enough to be able to look into her eyes when he demanded an explanation.

As soon as he saw her eyes filled with longing, he made a different sort of demand. He kissed her. He demanded a chance to demonstrate the sparks she wanted. He intended it to last only long enough to determine if she would kiss him back. When her response was immediately evident, he lost any sense of how long he should kiss her. Fortunately, he found he was not at all concerned to have no deadline or purpose. He simply enjoyed the moment and the soft hair down her back getting tangled in his fingers.

He ended the kiss only when he knew he was in danger of enjoying it too much. William took a moment to recover, to clear his head. Once he'd regained full use of his brain, he still couldn't understand what was happening. "Kay," he said, "why are you... *are* you thinking about canceling the wedding?"

She shook her head fervently.

"But you were?"

She tipped her head to the side, not really nodding but confirming that she had been.

"But now... what just happened?" He stared hard. She was going to have to communicate with actual words this time.

"I... I didn't know you could do that." Her voice carried a sigh of wonder.

William needed to explore that statement to be certain the relationship was back on track. He preferred not to have her elaborate on the doubts that he was man enough to make her feel anything. But if she wanted to describe exactly how wrong she'd been, he could probably let her talk for a while. He didn't know how to word the question to get her to focus on the positive.

"I was afraid we've been friends too long for you to think of me any other way," Kay said, before he asked anything.

It was good to know he didn't have any glaring shortcomings. It was only because they'd been friends so long that... "Wait a minute," William said as he got his brain the rest of the way around her explanation. "Are you telling me that when you said we needed to test the chemistry, you meant *I* needed..." The thought was too unbelievable to finish.

Kay nodded at him as though she didn't understand why that was surprising.

Clearly she needed more proof. He moved in to claim another kiss. This time she pushed him away. He didn't mind – at least not too much – because she seemed reluctant.

"You do want to marry me," she said.

"Why do you say it like it was uncertain? I've been saying it for months."

"You haven't said it like this before." Her eyes floated to his mouth and hovered there.

William accepted the invitation one more time before he stepped back to arm's length. They did have two suddenly long weeks before they tied the knot. He kept a tight hold on her hands. "And this is okay with you?" he asked. "All the chemistry is fine on your end?"

Her mouth wrestled with a smile before she managed to say, "You're the one who said we should be friends."

"When?"

"You know, back when…"

William wasn't sure he wanted to continue this discussion. It sounded as though it might hinge on bad decisions and missed opportunities on his part. Better not to dwell on the past. "I'm sorry you wasted time on that résumé," he said. "You don't need it now, right?"

She smiled. "I have never been happier to find out I wasted time."

Epilogue

The wedding was simple and practical. There were no decorations in the church, except for the small bouquets held by each of Annie's girls. Kay wore a basic knee-length dress. It was white with yellow ribbons on the sleeves the same shade as the girls' dresses. She found it the first time she looked for a dress, the day after William first kissed her.

Kay's dad and stepmom flew in from Seattle to be there. He congratulated her warmly with no hint that he disapproved of William. It was nice since he definitely disapproved of her choice to move in with him. Even better was watching him interact with Will and Pete like a grandfather and not like they reminded him of a lost daughter, though they still did. He had moved forward in his grief.

Despite the short ceremony, Kay's cheeks felt a little sore from all the smiling by the time they arrived at Annie and Jake's house.

"Do we have to go in?" William asked. "Couldn't we just take the boys home and avoid the party?"

"You're the one who told Annie she could put something together."

"Cake. I said she could put together a cake."

Kay laughed again, ignoring those tired muscles. "I was there," she said, "and I believe your exact words were 'Sure. Go crazy.'"

"I see God has blessed me with a wife whose memory is way too good."

"Come on." Kay opened her door. "She's going to feed us. I remember when you used to pretend that was the only reason you came over here."

"It's still the best reason," William said as he also got out of the car.

Annie hadn't gone crazy. There were decorations in the kitchen only, but all over the kitchen. She may have passed the crazy baton to her daughters because there were white ribbons tied onto nearly everything within four feet of the floor. The beanbags were pushed aside to make room for a small kids' table in the quiet room. Bailey looked very proud of herself helping Will with his lunch and giving him constant adult-sounding reminders to stay on his chair.

Then the cake came out. It wasn't fancy. It had Congrats spelled out in candy, which was a big hit with everyone except William and Annie's mom.

Diana wasn't terribly harsh, but she said, "That's not exactly an elegant wedding cake."

"Mom, it's for William. When has he ever been elegant?"

Diana sent an apologetic glance at Kay, who didn't know if she was apologizing for the cake or because her son wasn't elegant enough. The latter was unlikely, but it was a funny thought. Or maybe it wasn't that funny. Maybe Kay was only amused because it was already her favorite day ever.

"Cake is supposed to taste good," William said. "What it looks like isn't that important since we're going to hack it to pieces anyway."

His mom frowned slightly. "We're going to *slice* it."

"Into little pieces." William pointed somewhere near the center of the cake. "I'll take that one."

Now Annie frowned at him. "You'll have to wait until I get there then. I'm not cutting out the middle of the cake right now."

"I can wait."

Will got the first slice since it was also his birthday. Everyone sang to him while his eyes tried to eat the cake held out of his reach.

All the kids were served before the newlyweds. Kay had only eaten half her slice – it was a rich chocolate that deserved to be eaten slowly – when Ariana came into the kitchen with crumbs on her face. "I'm done," she said. "Is it time for presents now?"

Annie put down her cake to clean her daughter's hands and face, then chased a couple of smaller kids with sticky fingers. Will unwrapped a few new toys and Kay figured that was what Ariana meant when she mentioned presents. But then the two older girls brought out a stack of gifts in silvery wedding paper and set them in front of Kay and William.

"You weren't supposed to get us presents," Kay said. Annie and Jake were giving them a reception and the others had traveled and/or taken time off work. That was enough.

Patrick Donovan leaned forward to address his daughter. "You don't get gifts because you ask for them or even because you deserve them. You get gifts when people who love you want to celebrate an important event." He smiled but tipped his head sternly. "Let us celebrate."

Kay opened the first present with the unexpected feeling that it would be selfish not to enjoy it. Her new in-laws had gotten them a photo album. It had a lilac cover and a huge stack of extra pages for it.

"I expect a lot of memories in there by this time next year," Diana said.

Cliff addressed Kay in a stage whisper. "If you just remember to take some pictures, I know someone who will be happy to help you organize them."

His comment got a few laughs. It made Kay feel better about what was a nice present but also seemed a little like a homework assignment.

The present from Annie and Jake was a wok. "You said you wanted to try one," Annie said, looking at Kay for approval.

"I did say that. I think I'd like to watch William try, too."

He sighed next to her.

His mom said, "You're not still hopeless in the kitchen after all the work Kay has put into you?"

"I am."

"No, he's not." Kay smiled teasingly at William. "He's not hopeless. But he's not good either."

The last present was from Kay's dad. She lifted the lid from the box and gasped at a set of beautiful crystal hummingbirds nestled in tissue paper. "These were my mom's," she said. "I was never allowed to touch them." Her finger reverently and very lightly skimmed one of the wings. She wasn't sure she was allowed to touch them now.

"Your mom would want you to have those," Patrick said. "And she'd want you to spend the next several years trying to keep your children from breaking them."

Kay laughed until a crowd of children came over for a closer look at the fragile birds. She wanted to hide them away and realized that her mom had been generous to even let her look at them. She tipped the box gently so the kids could see, then put the lid back on before anyone asked to touch one.

"I know that's a gift mostly for Kay," Patrick said to William, "but when I considered that I was already giving you my daughter… well, there wasn't anything that could improve on that."

William nodded and reached for Kay's hand. "I absolutely did get the best gift today."

"The wok?" she asked.

"Yes, the wok. In fact," he paused to send her a wink, "we should go home and try it out right now."

She held his hand tighter to keep him in his chair. "We're not leaving in the middle of our party."

William broke into a falsetto. "It's my party and I'll leave if I want to, leave if I want to…"

The adults chuckled.

The younger kids were playing with Will's new toys.

Michael had fallen asleep with his cowboy hat covering half his face.

Bailey, who had probably never heard the song, gave her uncle a very strange look.

"It's a song," he explained to her.

She continued to stare at him. She said seriously, "You haven't opened the present from me yet."

"We're not leaving," William assured her. "I was kidding."

"Did you get us something?" Kay put excitement in her voice to make up for William.

"I *made* it," Bailey said. She ran towards the stairs, presumably to retrieve her present.

Kay leaned closer to William and whispered in his ear. "The boys will need naps soon. That's when we can leave."

He turned his head before she got away to give her a quick kiss of appreciation. Her cheeks might never recover from all the smiling. She was certain she had gotten the best gift. From now on, people would look at her and William with Will and Pete and see a family. And they would be right.

Thanks for reading!
If you enjoyed this book, please consider supporting the author by writing a review. Did you miss the companion short story? Read about Annie and Jake starting here: http://tinyurl.com/ybu6glvk

You might also like…

Said and Unsaid (Coffee and Donuts #1)

Alexa Fenley has some complicated relationships in her life. With her mom, she's trying to keep her temper. With her dad, she's trying to avoid any subject more emotionally charged than what one would write on a postcard. And with her sister, she's just trying.

Now Alexa has met someone new. She's trying to get to know him, trying to stop herself from falling too hard too fast, and trying not to let him know what she thinks of his name. But it's possible that this new relationship isn't nearly as complicated as Alexa thinks it is.

Sofie Waits (Coffee and Donuts #2)

Amber was Sofie's first friend at a new school, and they've been inseparable ever since. She's been the source of countless laughs and occasional dares. She supported Sofie through college and carried her through her mom's battle with cancer. But if Amber is her rock, Austin is Sofie's hard place. He's the only guy she's ever loved. She can't tell anyone because he's also Amber's brother.

Sofie has spent eleven years trapped between her feelings for Austin and her loyalty to Amber, who would be horrified to find out about those feelings. Now something has happened, something that means Sofie's feelings for Austin are no longer a secret. Sofie can't avoid the fallout forever, and it might not be anything like she expected.

A Perfectly Good Man (Coffee and Donuts #3)

Heidi Ray has a decision to make. It's a decision she probably should have made before she accepted the engagement ring. Tyler McAlston had the ring on her finger before she had a chance to think it through. But Tyler is a good man. Why wouldn't she want to marry him?

Unfortunately, Tyler isn't the only person in Heidi's life making her think. Heidi can get along with nearly anyone. She is starting to realize, however, that true happiness sometimes requires more than simply getting along. After much prayer and reflection, several of Heidi's relationships will begin to look different.

Not Complicated (Coffee and Donuts #4)

Molly's friends think she should be dating her friend Daniel. Molly's mom thinks they'll make the perfect couple. And Daniel's young daughter thinks they should just hurry up and get married already.

It might not be that simple though. Molly is getting a little tired of explaining why a romantic relationship with Daniel would be too complicated. But when Daniel admits that he wants what everyone else wants for them, staying friends no longer feels like the simplest option.

Andrew's Key (Stories From Hartford #1)

Talk around Hartford is that the old Hilson house is haunted. Its new owner, Rebecca Hilson, doesn't believe that. She's more concerned with the decades of junk that has accumulated and for which she is now responsible. She doesn't know what to do with any of it or even how to approach sorting through it all.

Her new neighbor, Andrew Lately, is happy to offer some words of wisdom and the help of his grandson, Charlie, to get her started. Charlie makes it clear right away that he is interested in more than helping Rebecca move boxes. She doesn't know if she can return those feelings. In fact, recent events have made her question her ability to feel much of anything.

Will Charlie's patience pay off or will it take a real ghost to help Rebecca understand the nature of love?

Jealousy & Yams (Stories From Hartford #2)

Luke Foster has been accused of being too nice for his own good. He enjoys being helpful though and never thought it was a problem until he met Summer. Now he believes she feels indebted to him, and it isn't gratitude he wants from her.

Summer Slough feels guilty for using Luke. She also feels an attraction to him that she doesn't know how to handle. It's beginning to look as though her mistakes and inexperience will keep them apart.

Lucky for both of them, Hartford's annual Yam Fest is right around the corner. The community event has a way of bringing people together... maybe even Summer and Luke.

Collecting Zebras (Stories From Hartford #3)
Angel Melling is determined to find a husband. The long held goal has recently morphed into an obsession. Being the new girl in a small town does have some advantages though. Angel quickly catches the eye of several of Hartford's eligible bachelors.

Her quest for a husband appears to be on the right track as she embarks on the most active dating of her life. But as the guys are ruled out one after another, Angel begins to fear that she'll run out of options. Will Angel find a guy who meets all the criteria for her happily ever after?

The Christmas Project (Stories From Hartford #4)
Hartford is full of small-town Christmas traditions and Gaby Bryant puts herself in the center of all of them. She loves Christmas and she loves things that stay the same. She spends most of the season engaged in one project after another, all intended to squeeze joy and beauty into the holiday. The fact that her friend Owen only reluctantly joins her preparations somehow adds to her fun.

But this year Owen has a project of his own. He wants to convince Gaby that not all change is bad and that if she'd stop thinking of him as "only" a friend, Christmas could be a whole lot merrier.

More books by Amanda Hamm

Hearts on the Window (Stories From Hartford #0.5)
The 4th Floor Lounge
Weathering Evan
Meet Cute: 5 Romantic Short Stories
Beyond Wisherton
Back to Wisherton

For more information visit amandahammbooks.com.
Thanks again.

www.ingramcontent.com/pod-product-compliance
Lightning Source LLC
Chambersburg PA
CBHW031317170626
46807CB00002B/453